Enrollment Form

☐ *Yes!* I WANT TO BE A *PRIVILEGED WOMAN*.
Enclosed is one *PAGES & PRIVILEGES*™ Proof of
Purchase from any Harlequin or Silhouette book currently for
sale in stores (Proofs of Purchase are found on the back pages
of books) and the store cash register receipt. Please enroll me
in *PAGES & PRIVILEGES*™. Send my Welcome Kit and FREE
Gifts -- and activate my FREE benefits -- immediately.

More great gifts and benefits to come.

NAME (please print)

ADDRESS   **APT. NO**

CITY   **STATE**   **ZIP/POSTAL CODE**

PROOF OF PURCHASE ONLY

**NO CLUB!
NO COMMITMENT!**
*Just one purchase brings
you great Free Gifts and
Benefits!*

Please allow 6-8 weeks for delivery. Quantities are limited. We reserve the right to
substitute items. Enroll before October 31, 1995 and receive one full year of benefits.

Name of store where this book was purchased_____

Date of purchase_____

Type of store:

    ☐ Bookstore   ☐ Supermarket   ☐ Drugstore

    ☐ Dept. or discount store (e.g. K-Mart or Walmart)

    ☐ Other (specify)_____

Which Harlequin or Silhouette series do you usually read?

_____

Complete and mail with one Proof of Purchase and store receipt to:

U.S.: *PAGES & PRIVILEGES*™, P.O. Box 1960, Danbury, CT 06813-1960

Canada: *PAGES & PRIVILEGES*™, 49-6A The Donway West, P.O. 813,
North York, ON M3C 2E8

SR-PP5B

▼ DETACH HERE AND MAIL TODAY! ▼

Fabulous Fathers

"I received a letter informing me that Emily is my daughter,"

Jon told her.

Alicia's head pounded and her only thought was to protect the daughter she loved, the daughter she wouldn't let anyone else lay claim to. She couldn't think with Jonathan Wescott standing so close. "Please leave."

"Alicia…"

"And don't talk to me as if you know me. You don't. Now leave my house."

Any charm she thought he might have, the gentleness she'd glimpsed as he'd talked to her daughter, was gone. His eyes were shuttered, his expression cold, his voice dangerous as he said, "She's my daughter and I intend to see her."

Their gazes locked in a battle of wills; she wouldn't look away. Finally he crossed to the door and brushed by her, his arm grazing hers. And as upset as she was, the contact still jolted her.

Dear Reader,

This month, take a walk down the aisle with five couples who find that a MAKE-BELIEVE MARRIAGE can lead to love that lasts a lifetime!

Beloved author Diana Palmer introduces a new LONG, TALL TEXAN in *Coltrain's Proposal*. Jeb Coltrain aimed to ambush Louise Blakely. Her father had betrayed him, and tricking Louise into a fake engagement seemed like the perfect revenge. Until he found himself wishing his pretend proposal would lead to a real marriage.

In Anne Peters's *Green Card Wife*, Silka Olsen agrees to marry Ted Carstairs—in name only, of course. Silka gets her green card, Ted gets a substantial fee and everyone is happy. Until Silka starts having thoughts about Ted that aren't so practical! This is the first book in Anne's FIRST COMES MARRIAGE miniseries.

In *The Groom Maker* by Debut author Lisa Kaye Laurel, Rachel Browning has a talent for making grooms out of unsuspecting bachelors. Yet, *she's* never a bride. When Trent Colton claims he's immune to matrimony, Rachel does her best to make him her own Mr. Right.

You'll also be sure to find more love and laughter in *Dream Bride* by Terri Lindsey and *Almost A Husband* by Carol Grace.

And don't miss the latest FABULOUS FATHER, Karen Rose Smith's *Always Daddy*. We hope you enjoy this month's selections and all the great books to come.

Happy Reading!

Anne Canadeo
Senior Editor, Silhouette Romance

Please address questions and book requests to:
Silhouette Reader Service
U.S.: 3010 Walden Ave., P.O. Box 1325, Buffalo, NY 14269
Canadian: P.O. Box 609, Fort Erie, Ont. L2A 5X3

ALWAYS DADDY

Karen Rose Smith

All my best,
Karen Rose Smith

Silhouette
ROMANCE™
Published by Silhouette Books
America's Publisher of Contemporary Romance

To Kenny with love.
May fate be kind as you pursue your dreams.
We're proud of you.

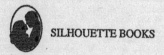 SILHOUETTE BOOKS

ISBN 0-373-19102-2

ALWAYS DADDY

This edition published by arrangement with Harlequin Books S.A.

® and TM are trademarks of Harlequin Books S.A., used under license. Trademarks indicated with ® are registered in the United States Patent and Trademark Office, the Canadian Trade Marks Office and in other countries.

Printed in U.S.A.

Books by Karen Rose Smith

Silhouette Romance

*Adam's Vow #1075
*Always Daddy #1102

Silhouette Special Edition

Abigail and Mistletoe #930

Published under the pseudonym Kari Sutherland

Silhouette Romance

Heartfire, Homefire #973

Silhouette Special Edition

Wish on the Moon #741

*Darling Daddies

KAREN ROSE SMITH

lives in Hanover, Pennsylvania, with her husband, an elementary school librarian, and their son, a recent college graduate. A former English teacher, she says writing and related activities take up most of her time, but she enjoys relaxed evenings at home with her husband and son, time alone with her husband and long conversations with friends.

Karen has read romances since she was a teenager precisely because they end with happily-ever-after. She thinks everyone needs an escape from time to time. She's thrilled to be writing under her real name for Silhouette. She formerly wrote under the pseudonym Kari Sutherland. Readers can write to Karen at P.O. Box 1545, Hanover, PA 17331.

Jonathan Wescott on Fatherhood...

Dear Emily,

I know I wasn't around when you were born, when you blessed the world with your first smile, when you took your first step, when you started your first day of kindergarten. All these years, I didn't know I had a wonderful little girl like you.

But now I do.

I will read you stories, give you piggyback rides and hug you every chance I get. I guarantee that when you talk to me, I will listen. Because I love you.

As you grow, I will answer your questions as honestly as I can, wipe your tears and try to make you smile. When you're old enough to think about boys, I will warn you, probably interfere and ruthlessly interrogate anyone you choose to date. Because I love you.

I promise you I will be the best dad I know how to be.

Always,

Daddy

Prologue

Jonathan Wescott read the letter a second time, not believing the words on the white linen stationery. His hand shook as he looked up at his closest friend and attorney. "My God, how could Cecile have done this to me?"

"From what her lawyer told me, she didn't know she was pregnant until after she got to Philadelphia," Adam Hobbs explained as he sat on the corner of the mahogany desk, his voice calm, yet his concern for his friend evident.

Jon whisked the letter in front of Adam's nose. "She says she told her lawyer I was dead and put the baby up for adoption because she knew I'd never let her put her career before a child. Am I such an ogre that she couldn't at least tell me?"

Adam scanned Jon's six-foot-two athletic stature. "Of course not. You just never realized exactly how selfish Cecile was. She knew you'd want to keep the child, and she'd always be tied to you and the baby if you did. She didn't want that responsibility.''

"And now she's dead and I've missed five years of my daughter's life!" Jon restrained the anger that rolled through him, threatening to explode. He swore viciously and swung around to stare at the Los Angeles skyline from Adam's seventh-story window as he realized that if Cecile hadn't been killed, he might never have known he had a daughter. *A daughter!*

A moment later, he felt Adam's hand on his shoulder. They'd been friends since college and understood each other well. Although Adam's specialty was corporate law and he handled Jon's business matters, he advised Jon on personal matters, too. "Besides assuaging Cecile's guilt, Jon, this letter's a gift. If she hadn't written it and left it with her attorney, you could have missed *more* than five years of your daughter's life."

Though Cecile's death was a shock, Jon wasn't surprised it had happened in her red sports car. He'd constantly worried about her penchant for speed in that vehicle...as well as her drive to get to the top in her profession. She'd left L.A. for a position in the East because she'd decided furthering her career by becoming vice president of a cosmetics company was more important than their relationship. Today he'd learned that she also considered her career more important than their child.

Adam dropped his hand to his side. "She left you more than the letter. Apparently her guilt got the best of her when she was on her deathbed. She left you blood samples."

Jon faced his friend. "I don't understand."

"If a DNA typing lab has the blood sample of the mother, child and alleged father, paternity can be determined with practical certainty. On her order, Cecile's attorney had her blood samples sent to a respected and reliable lab in Pittsburgh.''

Jon wondered if Cecile had left the letter and blood samples because she'd once cared or because, as Adam suspected, guilt had eaten at her.

Adam continued, ''I did some checking after her lawyer called me. I felt I should know the facts about the adoption so I could prepare you.''

But Jon hadn't let Adam prepare him. As usual, he'd cut off his friend's preamble and platitudes and ordered him to cut to the bottom line. That's when Adam had handed Jon the letter from Cecile, the letter she'd directed her lawyer to open on her death. The enormity of the information enclosed was starting to sink in.

His jaw set, his broad shoulders straight, Jon faced the circumstances head-on. ''What did you find out?''

Adam picked up the notes on his desk. ''The couple who adopted your daughter took her home the day after she was born. They adopted privately for a reason. Alicia Fallon was twenty-two—her husband was fifty-two. The PI's report said her husband had a low sperm count. And with him that age, they would have had a problem going through an agency. They also didn't want to wait the years it might have taken through normal channels.''

Jon paced across the oriental rug. ''I never could understand a match with that kind of age difference. What could they possibly have in common? When my daughter's sixteen—''

''It won't matter, Jon. Patrick Fallon died of a heart attack two years ago. Alicia Fallon is a widow.''

Jon stood still. Thank God he had money. He'd learned at an early age that it was a persuasive tool, that it could buy him information and services and bend minds to his way of thinking. "Where does this Fallon woman live?"

"Camp Hill, Pennsylvania."

Jon raked his fingers through his thick black hair. "Draw up papers for visitation rights for now. I want to file for custody but first I need to know the situation." Crossing to the desk, he lifted the receiver on Adam's intercom and buzzed the lawyer's secretary. "Suz, it's Jon. Get me the first flight out to Pennsylvania. Find the closest airport to Camp Hill. That's two words?"

Adam nodded, then frowned. "Jon, you can't just go racing out there."

"Why not?"

"Because you don't want to scare this woman. You don't want to put your chances for custody in jeopardy."

"Save the arguments for boardroom negotiations, Adam. I'm going to see my daughter and the sooner the better."

Chapter One

Alicia Fallon pushed a lock of her blond hair away from her cheek and flipped on the printer. As it warmed up, she turned back to her computer, studying the logo she'd designed. Smiling, she mentally patted herself on the back. It was good work and a large account. Starting her own business with the insurance money she'd received after Patrick's death had been a risk. She wasn't usually a woman who took risks, but this one had paid off.

The sound of Emily's laughter drifted down the short flight of stairs from the kitchen into Alicia's office. She liked to leave the door open when she wasn't assisting clients so she could hear Emily's squeals and chatter as she played and spoke to Gertie. If the door was open, Emily knew she could come down and visit with her mother. This split-level was perfect for them, although Alicia had been sad to leave Patrick's house where she'd found comfort and safety for the first time in her life.

The single ding of her office doorbell alerted her to her new client arriving. He'd called the day before to set up an appointment to discuss a promotional brochure for a charity benefit his company was planning. She'd forgotten to ask him who had recommended her graphic design business.

When Alicia went to the door and saw the man standing there, she took a step back. He was tall and dark, with too stern a jaw to be called handsome. The male musk scent of his cologne wafted through the screen along with the April breeze. His deep baritone on the phone hadn't prepared her for his imposing presence. Maybe it was the coal blue classic striped suit that made his shoulders seem so broad, his legs so long.

She took a deep breath and opened the screen door. Putting on her cool, professional face, she asked, "Mr. Wescott?"

He smiled, the harsh line of his jaw seeming to soften. But his piercing green eyes kept her on guard. That was her usual response to men who exuded power, dominance, and a hint of arrogance in their demeanor. She preferred pussycats. Or maybe she was simply afraid of tigers. Life had taught her to be.

"Yes, and you're Mrs. Fallon?" he extended his hand.

Impeccable manners, too. As soon as his hand enfolded hers, her gaze was drawn up to his. A tremor ran through her, an excited little tremor that was as foreign as the German she'd tried to master in college. Swallowing, she pulled her hand from his grasp, crossed the room, and sat in the chair behind her desk.

Motioning to the upholstered chair across from her, she asked, "How can I help you?"

He seemed to hesitate a moment. After scanning the office with a quick sweep of his eyes over the mauve and powder blue flowered decor as well as the room beyond where her workroom was set up, he appraised her. She could feel his evaluation from the tip of her blond head, clear down her pink blouse and slacks to the ivory flats she'd slipped on this morning. She fought the urge to pull her chair further into her desk.

He seemed to hesitate for a moment before he took the seat she offered. Reaching into his inner jacket pocket, he pulled out a program, a paper with updated information, and an invitation. He laid them in front of her. "This is what we did last year. Can you come up with something similar for this year?"

Wescott Enterprises announces its charity gala, she read. Rolling her chair closer to the desk, she examined the front and inside of the folded program. "This is straightforward. How many are you considering?"

"Six hundred programs. I'll need two hundred fifty invitations, too. Black on off-white. Understated."

Turning the program over, she noticed the address. California? She frowned. "Mr. Wescott..."

"Jon."

Her gaze bumped into his. Using his first name seemed too...familiar. "This event takes place in Los Angeles?"

He nodded. "That's where Wescott Industries is located."

Even if his company was small, she thought, surely a secretary could take care of something like this. "But you want to have them printed here?"

His shoulders straightened slightly and the nerve along his jaw worked. "I'm in Camp Hill on business. I don't know how long it will take. While I'm here, I thought I'd take care of some odds and ends. Is there a problem?"

Maybe he was as much a perfectionist as she was and liked to take care of every detail himself. "No, I suppose not. How soon do you need them?"

"As soon as you can get them done. The date this year is June 20."

That was over two months away. She still couldn't understand why he was having them printed here, unless as owner of the company he was involved in every detail and had to approve it. "This only involves typesetting. If I get them to the printer by Friday, we're probably looking at the middle of next week. When I get an estimate—"

Clatter and clamor interrupted Alicia as Emily pounded down the stairs, an oatmeal cookie in each hand. "Want one, Mommy? Gertie said—"

The child stopped midstaircase when she saw Jon Wescott. She sank onto the step and looked to her mother for what to do next.

Alicia held out her arms. "It's okay, honey. Come here."

Emily grinned and scampered down the remaining steps, zipped past Jon and climbed onto Alicia's lap. Munching on one cookie, Emily offered the other to her mother while glancing at Jon beneath lowered lashes.

Jon was stunned. Not just by his child, but also by Alicia. He hadn't expected to meet her in her home, for one thing. He also hadn't expected such a beautiful face, wary blue eyes and long blond hair that looked as soft as her voice sounded. Her tailored blouse in no way detracted from her femininity. Everything about Alicia Fallon was utterly feminine and appealing. He was used to dealing with sharper, more...sophisticated women.

And her daughter, *his* daughter, was enchanting. Her dark brown hair curled around her ears and cheeks. Her green eyes were the same color as his. As cookie crumbs collected around her mouth, he leaned forward and smiled.

"Are oatmeal cookies your favorite snack?" he asked, urged by the need to make some kind of contact with his daughter.

Emily wriggled on her mother's lap. "I like lollipops, too."

Alicia gave her daughter a hug. "Too much. I have to ration her."

Emily slid from her mother's lap and came to stand beside Jon. "I can have one after lunch. But I can't run with it in my mouth."

Jon pretended seriousness. "That's important to remember."

Emily nodded soberly. "Mommy says so."

"Honey, why don't you go see what Gertie's doing," Alicia suggested with a nod up the stairs.

Emily held on to the arm of Jon's chair and swayed back and forth. "She's foldin' clothes."

"Think you can help her?"

Emily sighed a little-girl sigh. "I guess." She peered over the top of her mother's desk at the cookie. "Are you gonna eat that?"

"After I'm finished talking business with Mr. Wescott."

Emily took a last look at Jon and darted up the stairs.

Jon stared at the back of the child's denim overalls. "She's adorable."

"I think so."

Alicia's smile was uninhibited and warm, and she'd lost her aura of reserve. She'd been so natural with Emily, so attentive. As if no one or nothing could be more important at that moment. She hadn't been at all impatient that Emily had intruded into a business meeting. He could imagine what Cecile would have done. Of course, she wouldn't have had a child at her place of business.

"Does she bring you snacks often?"

Alicia became coolly polite again. "Are you asking if I'm constantly interrupted?"

He kept his voice friendly, though impatience and getting a glimpse of his daughter prompted him to tell her why he was really here. "She's a pleasant interruption."

Seeing that he wasn't criticizing, Alicia relaxed. "She's in kindergarten in the mornings. I have a neighbor who comes here to watch her in the afternoon. When I leave the door open, Emily knows she can come down. I forgot to close it after you came in."

Had she experienced a physical reaction to him as he had to her? Jon wondered. Is that why she'd forgotten the open door? "How long have you been in business?"

Alicia picked up his sample invitation, examining it as she answered, "Two years. How did you find out about Designs For You?"

Jon shifted in his chair, feeling guilty for deceiving her. But after Adam realized he couldn't dissuade Jon from the trip, his lawyer had drummed into his head that he couldn't just blurt out the truth. After discovering what Alicia did for a living, this seemed like a good way to make initial contact. And he did plan to contract for her services.

"The yellow pages," he answered. Thank goodness he'd checked her listing before he called. He demanded honesty from everyone he dealt with from his personal life to his business encounters. He didn't want to lie to this woman.

Alicia leaned back in her swivel chair. "It's amazing how many clients I get that way." Studying the program this time, she said, "I can call you with an estimate tomorrow."

"I'd rather stop by."

Her gaze snapped to his. "Pardon me?"

He had to make this sound logical and practical. "I'm staying at the Excelsior. I have a few appointments tomorrow and will be in and out. I can easily just stop in around one if that fits into your schedule."

She flipped her appointment calendar to the following day and glanced at a list on her desk. "I think I can fit in working on a proof tomorrow morning. Do you want a similar type style?"

"Can you show me the choices?" He didn't care a whit about type style, but he didn't want to leave yet.

Taking a folder from the shelves behind her, she opened it and removed two style sheets. "Number twenty is the closest to what you have now."

When he took the laminated sheet from her, their fingers brushed. He raised his head and met the startled recognition in her eyes. A moment later, her lashes came down hiding her reaction. In a jerky movement, she swiveled around, and took a binder from the shelves.

Not meeting his gaze, she flipped it open and pointed to an off-white linen paper sample. "Is this what you have in mind for the invitations?"

"That's exactly what I have in mind." Actually what he had in mind would probably send her scurrying away. Remembering why he'd come, he suddenly realized how awkward and complicated an attraction to this woman could be. Besides the fact that she wasn't his type any more than small-town living was his environment, Emily was his first concern. Yet seeing his daughter with Alicia...

He needed to talk to Adam.

Now.

Standing abruptly, he asked, "Tomorrow at one will work for you?"

If she was surprised by his sudden decision to leave, she didn't show it. She answered politely, "I'll pencil you in."

He nodded but couldn't help extending his hand once more. "It was a pleasure meeting you."

She looked at his hand, then gave it the quickest shake in history. He still felt her hand's warmth, its fragility, its softness. In more turmoil than he'd thought possible, he said goodbye and strode out the door.

Once outside, he tugged down his tie. Alicia Fallon and her daughter were going to complicate his life more than he'd ever imagined.

Then he reminded himself—Emily was *his* daughter.

"She's not what I expected," Jon told Adam on the phone an hour later.

"What did you expect?"

"I don't know. Maybe I hoped I'd find something wrong. A bad situation. She loves Emily as if she were her own."

"Emily is her own. Legally speaking. And probably emotionally, too, if I understand you correctly. I have the letter of intent to file for visitation typed up. Should I send it?"

Jon glanced around the efficiency suite he'd be calling home for two weeks, maybe more. "Yes. I'm going to tell her tomorrow. I don't think she'll do something stupid like taking Emily and running off."

"Are you sure?"

Jon thought about Alicia's cool reserve but remembered the expression on her face when she hugged her daughter. "I'm guessing."

"Are you going to tell her you want joint custody?"

Remembering Emily sitting on Alicia's lap, the obvious love between them, he swore. "I don't know yet. I'm going to play it by ear. This is sticky. If anyone knows that, you should." Not so long ago Adam's ex-wife had felt threatened by Adam's wanting joint custody and she'd taken their two daughters out of the country.

"If you intend to file, you need a Pennsylvania lawyer to handle it for you," Adam explained. "Let me give you a name. Do you have a pen?"

Jon copied down the name, address and number. Then more to himself than to Adam, he said, "I have to go ahead with this. Emily's my daughter."

"I know how you feel, Jon. But you have to be cautious. Does Mrs. Fallon know who you are?"

"What do you mean?"

"Does she know you own a multimillion dollar newspaper enterprise?"

"No. Why?"

"Because if you sue for visitation, she could go for an ample amount of child support."

"I'll want to give that to her anyway."

"Your fair share. With a good lawyer, she could get a lot more than that."

He'd come out here thinking money could solve this problem as it did most others. After meeting Alicia, he wasn't so sure. "Adam, I can't think about that now. I'll call you when I have new information."

"Good luck."

"Thanks. I have a feeling I'll need it."

The midday sun couldn't be brighter. Jon wondered why he never noticed its yellow brilliance in L.A. Maybe it had something to do with the smog. Or maybe he was indoors more than outdoors...when he wasn't traveling somewhere to look into buying a defunct newspaper, or helping to settle contract negotiations, or... How had his life become such a rat race?

Ever since his father died and he'd had to take over the infant empire, fulfilling his dad's dreams had become his focus, his reason for living. Now, that might have to change. He had a daughter. He still had trouble believing it at times.

When he rang the bell to Alicia's office, she didn't answer. Checking his watch, he realized he was fifteen minutes early. Should he go to the front door? Better yet, he'd rather look around. Hearing the squeal of a child, he followed the sound.

The yard wasn't large, but there was enough room for a clothesline, redwood picnic table and barbecue grill near the house, a swing set farther back, and in one corner an unfinished structure that looked like a wooden box with a slanted roof. Emily sat on the swing as Alicia pushed her. The child laughed, a pure sweet sound that rang out across the yard. As Alicia pushed, her shoulder-length hair swung in the breeze, shining like spun gold. Nothing could have prevented him from walking toward them, and he'd never been gripped by such an inclination to join in.

When Alicia saw him open the wooden gate and step within its boundaries, she frowned. The sunshine seemed to dim. Emily pointed to him and jumped from the swing.

He'd dressed casually today, hoping that would put Alicia more at ease. He caught her appraisal of his khakis and lightweight red windbreaker, and her interest heated his blood. She wore a white sweater coat over a dress with a slightly scooped neck and a gathered skirt. The small blue flowers dancing across the white background were the same color as her eyes.

Emily came right over to Jon, the hood to her nylon jacket flapping on her back. "Wanna swing?"

Jon checked out the white plastic seat. "I might break it."

"Nah. Mommy sits on it."

He crouched down to Emily's level. "Your mom's a lot lighter than I am."

"You can try the sliding board."

The apparatus was made for anyone under three feet tall. "Well, I'd really like to but maybe you can tell me what that is instead." He pointed to the partially finished structure.

"My playhouse! C'mon, I'll show you." Emily took off at a run.

Jon glanced at Alicia. She wasn't frowning anymore, but she wasn't smiling, either. Before she could intervene and send his daughter into the house, he followed the little girl across the yard.

Alicia came up beside him. "You don't have to do this."

He kept walking. "Does she play in it?"

"I won't let her. The boards are rough inside. The carpenter who was working on it was called back to work. He hasn't had time to finish it. At least he got it under cover. But the walls need to be paneled inside, and the shingles have to be attached. I can't paint the outside until that's done."

"You're going to do it?"

"Does that surprise you, Mr. Wescott?"

"Jon," he reminded.

Emily hopped up and down as they approached. "It has a window, and a door, just like our big house!"

Jon laughed. "I see. What are you going to put inside?"

"Furniture, of course," she answered in a very grown-up fashion.

He bit back a smile. "Of course."

Alicia placed her hands on her daughter's shoulders. "Time to go inside now. Tell Gertie I'll be in my office."

Emily waved at Jon as she ran across the yard to the back door. He waved back, determined to spend more time with her, determined to tell Alicia the truth.

Alicia walked toward her office. "I have everything ready. I think you'll be pleased with the estimates. The printer I use is reasonable."

Jon strode beside her, thinking about the best way to tell her about Emily. Strategy had always been his strong suit. What could he do to make Alicia Fallon be the most receptive?

Shrugging out of her sweater and hanging it on one of the three wooden pegs on the wall, Alicia then went straight to her desk to a manila folder lying there. He could tell she was organized. When she opened the folder and handed him her work, he knew she was precise and expert at what she did, too. The sample cover of the program was very much like last year's. Yet it was different. The Wescott logo was larger, making it a focal point. She'd also added a simple border of leaves at the two corners that framed the print. It was effective.

She sat in her chair as he sat across from her and said, "I took the liberty of adding the border. If you don't like it—"

"I like it. It gives the program some style, makes it less cut-and-dried."

"And the invitation?"

He smiled at her, appreciating the contours of her face, the cornflower blue of her eyes, her creamy skin emphasized by the delicate gold chain around her neck. "It's just right."

Alicia leaned back to put more distance between her and Jonathan Wescott's smile, a smile that created a sensation similar to riding a roller coaster car down a wild dip. She didn't understand why she was reacting to him this way. Her upbringing had taught her to be wary of men...domineering men like her father. He'd ordered, yelled, criticized, and in general had run everyone's lives. She'd married Patrick because he'd made her feel safe. This man made her feel anything *but* safe. The feelings he evoked were exciting...and dangerous.

Ria would say it was about time she was attracted to a man. Her twin sister reacted much differently to the world around her than Alicia did. Ria would take one look at Jonathan, roll her eyes, say "What a hunk," and...

"Have dinner with me tonight."

She couldn't have heard him correctly. "What?"

He smiled—a charming, boyish, melt-her-bones smile. "It's not fun eating meals alone when I travel. I'd appreciate the company."

Alicia wheeled her chair back another inch or so to escape his smile's effect. "That's not possible."

"What about tomorrow?"

"I spend my evenings with my daughter."

His gaze locked to hers. "All of them?"

"Yes."

Laying the folder on the desk, he asked, "You don't date?"

"My life is full, Mr. Wescott. I have a thriving business and a daughter whom I love to spend time with."

"Jon," he reminded, not giving up. "Certainly one dinner out wouldn't hurt."

"I don't think so."

"I can supply references." He smiled again, but this time it didn't reach his eyes.

"I've already prepared a casserole for supper."

"I can beat that. Steak, lobster... take your pick."

She'd been trying to let him down easily but he was more persistent than most. "No."

He blew out a breath and raked his hand through his hair. "You're not making this easy."

"What?"

"Alicia, I have something to discuss with you."

She didn't like the tone of his voice, the familiarity that led her to feel he knew more about her than she knew about him. "Anything you have to discuss, we can discuss here."

He frowned. "It's personal."

"I don't know you. How can it be personal?"

"It's about Emily."

A foreboding prickled through Alicia and she straightened in her chair. "What about Emily?"

Jonathan Wescott stood, paced to the steps while he looked up at the closed door, and rubbed his hand across his forehead. Turning around to face her, his expression serious, he said, "I received a letter. A letter from Cecile Braddock."

Alicia's heart hammered and she felt the color leave her face. "How do you know her?"

"Did you know Cecile died recently?"

A surge of relief swept through Alicia though she immediately felt guilty for it. "No, I didn't. But you said she sent you a letter..."

He moved close to the desk. "Cecile and I were involved five years ago. Last week my lawyer contacted me. After Cecile was in an automobile accident and knew she wouldn't recover, she left me a letter. There's no easy way to say this. The letter informed me that Emily is my daughter."

"No!"

"It's true."

"She said the father was dead. She said—"

"She lied."

Alicia's hands tightened around the arms of her chair. "How do I know *you're* not lying? You have no proof."

"I have the letter."

Her head pounded and her only thought was to protect the daughter she loved, the daughter she wouldn't let anyone else lay claim to. She couldn't think with Jonathan Wescott standing there, towering over her.

She stood and came around from behind the desk. "Please leave."

"Alicia..."

"And don't talk to me as if you know me. You don't. Please leave. If you don't, I'll call the police."

A hard edge to his voice made his words seem louder than they were. "You'll have to deal with this eventually."

She went to the door and waited.

Any charm she thought he might have, the gentleness she'd glimpsed as he'd talked to her daughter, was gone. His eyes were shuttered, his expression cold, his voice dangerous as he said, "She's my daughter and I intend to see her. I'll take this to court if I have to. I'll do whatever is necessary. If money is what you want, maybe we can settle this without going to court."

She blinked. "You think I'd sell my daughter?" she asked, anger mixed with astonishment making her voice rise.

"Of course not." He again raked his hand through his hair. "But I'm sure a monetary settlement can help us reach a solution."

"There is no solution. You keep your money, Mr. Wescott. And you stay away from Emily."

The lines of his jaw stiffened along with his posture. "That isn't possible. She's my daughter, too. If you won't be reasonable about this, get ready for the fight of your life."

Alicia's silence told him better than words that she didn't consider "reasonable" an option.

Taking a business card from his pocket, he snapped it on her desk. "If you don't call me within twenty-four hours, I'll take the next step, a less personal one."

Alicia still stood silently by the door, her expectation that he leave a palpable vibration in her office. She realized he was a force to be reckoned with, but he had to understand that she would protect and safeguard her daughter no matter what she had to do.

Their gazes locked in a battle of wills; she wouldn't look away. Finally he crossed to the door and brushed by her, his arm grazing hers. As upset as she was, the contact still jolted her. Hearing the screen door shut behind him, she closed her eyes.

She'd feared this day. Ever since the adoption. Yes, Emily knew she was adopted. Alicia and Patrick intended their daughter to know she was chosen and wanted badly. But Alicia had always feared that some day Cecile Braddock would realize she'd made a mistake, she'd realize she'd given up the most precious gift of her life.

Alicia shook and leaned against the door as tears welled up and ran over. She'd never expected to have to worry about a father, too.

Her legs suddenly felt weak and she slid down to the floor, crossing her arms over her aching heart. She would not lose Emily. She would not. She'd fight. She'd fight with everything she had, everything she could find.

The phone rang as her first sob broke loose. Alicia dropped her face into her hands and let the tears come as the phone continued to ring.

Chapter Two

Alicia's answering machine kicked on while she still had her face buried in her hands. At first she didn't register the caller's voice, but within seconds her sister's concern penetrated her anguish. "Alicia, are you okay? I had this funny feeling. You know what I mean. You've gotten it often enough, too. Are you there? Is Emily all right?"

Ria's voice urged Alicia to push herself to her feet. Crossing to the desk she picked up the receiver. "Ria, I'm here." Her voice was a hoarse whisper.

"What's wrong? Are you sick?" her twin asked with concern.

Taking a breath, she pulled herself together. "Sick at heart."

"What's happened?"

"A man came here and said he's Emily's father."

"But he's dead!"

Alicia ran her hand across her forehead. "Jonathan Wescott says Cecile Braddock lied."

"And?"

"He threatened to take us to court. He offered me money."

"Money?"

"I told him I didn't want his money and he should stay away from us. But I don't think he will." She remembered his twenty-four-hour deadline. "I have to call a lawyer." She'd find out what her rights were, then she'd face Jonathan Wescott armed for battle.

The following morning, Alicia paced Ria's office, her hands shoved deep into the pockets of her suit jacket. She'd called Tom Marsten, the lawyer who'd handled Emily's adoption. "I'm frightened, Ria. Tom believes Jonathan Wescott can get visitation rights on the strength of that letter alone. What chance do I have? What if I lose Emily?"

Ria's short, blond, blunt-cut hair swung along her cheek as she answered firmly, "You are *not* going to lose your daughter."

Throughout their lives, Ria had been the cheerleader, the rebel, the free spirit who'd kept Alicia from retreating into herself. "Thank you. You always say what I need to hear. I hope I'm doing the right thing meeting this man without Tom present. But Tom couldn't set up a meeting until next week and I know Jonathan Wescott wouldn't wait that long before taking some kind of action."

"It might be better this way, Sis. If Marsten were here, Wescott would want his lawyer present. They could hide what information they have and save it for a more opportune moment, like in court. Lawyers create an adversarial atmosphere from step one. This might be the best way to go. At least you'll find out his intentions."

Alicia had been grateful when Ria had offered her office, one of many in the business firm for which she worked, as a neutral meeting place. "I feel as if I'm going to jump out of my skin. What time is it?"

"Nine fifty-five. He might decide to be late just to rattle you."

As fear wound a tighter web around Alicia's heart, she stopped pacing long enough to respond, "He's already rattled me."

Jon found the office building easily. It was a five-story block-and-glass structure housing a roster of businesses. When Alicia Fallon had called him, she'd been icily polite and curt. But he didn't care. This meeting was all that mattered. His daughter was all that mattered.

He went to the suite number Alicia had given him. The name on the glass door announced—Fourstar Office Products. The receptionist looked up from her word processor as Jon approached. When he gave Alicia's name, the woman directed him down a hall to the third door on the left.

The name Ariana McKendall was on the door with the title, Account Manager, painted underneath. Jon pushed open the already ajar door and saw Alicia standing at the window, gazing out. He would recognize her blond hair and her ramrod straight posture anywhere. But when he caught a glimpse of the woman seated behind the desk, he blinked and examined her once more. She had Alicia's face! Her hair was more yellow-blond rather than the deep honey of Alicia's, and it was cut in a bob around her face rather than worn longer and flowing like the woman's who was standing at the window. But the resemblance was uncanny.

The blonde behind the desk saw him first. "Mr. Wescott?"

Alicia turned around. Her face was composed as she faced him. "Mr. Wescott, this is my sister, Ariana McKendall."

Ariana stood. "Mr. Wescott, if you don't mind, I'd like to sit in."

"Ria, that's not necessary," Alicia protested.

"I don't mind," he said curtly to them both. "Who is or isn't here won't change the facts. I'm Emily's father."

Ria pointed to the two chairs in front of the desk. "Why don't you have a seat."

Jon could tell this sister was used to being in charge, just as her bold, harlequin-patterned dress told him her tastes and Alicia's were different. Alicia sat, her knees tilted to one side in a ladylike position under her mint green linen skirt. She folded her hands in her lap. As Jon took the other chair, his suit coat brushed her arm. Her gaze smacked into his.

Her blue eyes were guarded. He wished he could say something to put her more at ease, but this wasn't an easy situation.

Once he was seated, Alicia spoke first. "Just because you say you're Emily's father doesn't make it so. What proof do you have?"

Jon had expected the inquiry. He withdrew a copy of Cecile's letter from his inside pocket and held it out to Alicia. "It's self-explanatory. You can keep that copy. The name of my lawyer and his number is attached in case you want to check to make sure what I say is true."

She was very careful not to let her fingers touch his, and that annoyed him, though he didn't understand why. As she read the letter, her hand tightened on the paper, her knuckles straining to almost white. She handed it to her sister. "That doesn't prove anything. If Cecile Braddock lied once, she could be lying again."

"People don't ordinarily leave lies with their wills," he countered.

"That depends," Ria argued. "It could be wishful thinking on her part."

Jon met Ria's implication head-on. "Cecile and I saw each other exclusively when she lived in Los Angeles."

"You can't be sure of that," Ria returned.

"I *knew* Cecile Braddock. I would be perceptive enough to know if someone else was in the picture. There was no one else." Cecile's job had consumed her. Jon knew she hadn't had time for anyone else; they barely had time for each other. He added, "The last time Cecile and I were together was at the end of September, a month before she left the West Coast. When's Emily's birthday?"

Alicia threw her sister a frightened look. "June 27."

Knowing the two sisters were calculating, too, he made his point. "The dates work."

Alicia's cheeks pinkened.

Ria challenged him. "But your theory doesn't necessarily work, Mr. Wescott. You can *think* you know someone. The best of us can be deceived, especially when our hearts are involved."

The woman's response was too vehement not to have come from personal experience. "That might be true for you. I always think with my head, not any other part of my anatomy." With a quick glance at Alicia, he noticed her flush had deepened. Ria seemed unaffected. "At any rate, your observation is meaningless. I'm willing to undergo paternity testing if necessary."

"I won't put Emily through that," Alicia argued.

"You might not have any choice." His boardroom voice was as sharp as steel.

Alicia's shoulders straightened. "I always have a choice. I will not do anything detrimental to Emily."

"If a judge orders the test, you will have no choice. All the test requires is a blood sample."

The seriousness of his intent must have sunk in because Alicia grew pale. "What do you want, Mr. Wescott?"

"For now, I want time with my daughter. I want to get to know her, and I want her to know I'm her father. Eventually I want specific visitation rights and possibly joint custody."

"No!"

He wished he could take the stricken look from Alicia's face, but he couldn't. "Yes. And I'll do whatever I have to do to get what I want. As I told you, I'm willing to be reasonable about a monetary settlement."

Alicia hopped out of her chair. "As I told you before, Mr. Wescott, your money is worthless to me. You can't buy me or my daughter. Have you even stopped to think about Emily? You talk about what *you* want. What about her? I will not have her life . . . disrupted . . . turned upside down. She's secure and she has a minimum of fears for a child her age. I won't have her scared, afraid you're going to take her away from me."

"Aren't they your fears, Alicia, not hers?" he asked calmly, though inside he was anything but calm.

"No," Alicia repeated as if the word could somehow stop him. "You have no right—"

He stood and faced her, not wanting to intimidate her, but wanting to show her she had to deal with him. "I'm going to prove I do."

Clasping her hands in front of her, she insisted, "I won't cooperate with you. I won't hurt Emily."

"If you don't cooperate, you will hurt Emily."

Determination settled around her mouth, between her brows. "We'll see about that. You want to go to court? Fine. We'll go to court. You're not going to threaten me with that. Anyone who knows anything about children would believe her best interests are to stay with me. I'm her mother."

He didn't want to hurt this woman, but he wouldn't give up his daughter. "You're her adoptive mother. I'm her natural father. My rights were ignored when she was born. They won't be again. If I don't hear from you or your lawyer by the end of the week defining some way we can come to terms on this, you'll hear from my lawyer. Good day, ladies." Jon strode out of the office, anger and fear burning in his gut.

Once he was in the hall, he turned back for a moment. Long enough to see Ria go to Alicia and put her arm around her sister's shoulders.

He turned away. He had an appointment to make. With a Pennsylvania lawyer.

Jon used the rowing machine in the hotel's gym more to relieve tension than to work out. Try as he would, he couldn't get the picture out of his head of Ria comforting Alicia. Or Alicia pushing Emily on the swing, or hugging her, or looking at her with enough love to prepare her for life. Too many parents didn't know where to begin to guide their kids. His father sure hadn't; he'd only known how to relate to adults—adults he could command, or use to get what he wanted. He'd used Jon the same way. If it hadn't been for his mother...

Cecile had used him, too. Dreaming of children with Cecile Braddock, Jon hadn't realized how much he'd cared for her until the day she told him her career was more important than he was and any future they might have. He'd felt betrayed and manipulated into a relationship he'd had every intention of forging into a strong marriage. But one person couldn't make a marriage, and as he discovered, Cecile had no intention of trying. She'd needed his contacts and his family's social status to further her career. And she'd done it.

He'd been bitter and angry until it had eaten away any joy he could find in life. Then somehow, after his father died and Jon had too much work to accomplish to take time to eat or sleep, he'd realized the anger and bitterness had faded, leaving caution and a defensive detachment in its wake. He got involved with women, but he never let his heart get involved, too. Never again.

He'd been rowing with such a feverish determination that the gym attendant gave him a warning glare. As the sweat dripped from Jon's brow, he slowed down and again saw Alicia's image in front of his eyes. From what he'd seen, she was a different type of woman from those he'd known. The anguish on her face when he'd said he might go after custody had twisted his heart.

Swearing, he stopped rowing. He thought about Alicia and her feelings, really thought about them, for the first time. How would he feel if he'd adopted and nurtured a child and someone charged into his life demanding time, rights, custody? He'd use every iota of strength he possessed to hold on tightly, to explore every option so he didn't have to give an inch.

Yes, he'd made an appointment with the lawyer Adam had recommended. But he suddenly realized that, at this point, a lawyer and decrees would only make Alicia more stubborn, more possessive, more determined to hold on to her daughter with both hands. And what would that do to Emily?

A few hours later, Jon stood at Alicia's front door rather than her office door. He rang the bell and waited.

When she came to the foyer and saw him, her sweetly curved mouth tightened to a disapproving frown. "We have nothing to discuss."

"I know you want to slam the door in my face. And I don't blame you. You think I'm trying to take something away from you. But that's not true."

"Not something. My daughter."

He tried a different tack, forcing his voice to remain calm. "You and I are intelligent enough to know that lawyers are going to complicate this."

She hesitated for a moment. "Exactly what do you want? I won't let you disrupt Emily's life."

"Then help me not to. Let's work something out between us that will benefit all of us."

Alicia shook her head. "You want to benefit yourself, Mr. Wescott. Are you really thinking about Emily at all, let alone me?"

"Let's go to dinner and discuss it." Before she could deny him without thinking about it, he pressed on. "A dinner can't hurt. Neither can talking." He saw fear flicker in her eyes. Unreasonably he didn't want her to fear him. He didn't want her to fear anyone. "What do you say?"

"I can't tonight. I promised Emily I'd take her for pizza."

"And you don't break your promises."

"Not if I can help it."

He wanted to go along with them. He wanted to get close to his daughter, and he also wanted to find out more about Alicia. She'd been reserved around him before she'd known what he wanted. Was she that way with everyone? "Tomorrow night, then."

"Let me think about it. I'll let you know."

If he backed off now, it might pay off in the long run. "I'll be waiting to hear from you." But he wouldn't wait too long.

Her hands were clutched in front of her, her forehead creased with worry. Before he knew where it came from, he found himself reassuring her. "Alicia, I don't want to harm you or Emily in any way."

"That remains to be seen."

Her walls were sturdily in place. Jon understood walls. He wondered about the reasons behind Alicia Fallon's.

Jon waited two days. He wasn't good at waiting, never had been. Finally, taking matters into his own hands, he went to a deli and had a picnic dinner prepared.

Walking up to Alicia's door again, he wondered if he should have bought fast food instead. Too late now. He felt more certain about the two-foot colorful stuffed parrot he'd brought for Emily. What kid wouldn't like it?

The sky was more gray than blue. The weather report had called for showers with the warmer weather, but hopefully not anytime soon. Checking his watch, Jon hoped he'd arrived just as Alicia had quit working but before she started supper. Ringing her front doorbell, his gut tightened. Tonight could make the difference between peace and hostility.

Alicia came to the door, her flowered blouse and peach split skirt making the day seem brighter. She saw the parrot and frowned. The tension inside him increased.

"I was going to call you later."

"To tell me . . ." he prompted.

"That I called your lawyer, Adam Hobbs. He assured me everything you've told me is true. I was going to accept your invitation to dinner."

She didn't sound happy about the decision. Jon lifted the deli bag and smiled, hoping to coax one from her. "I brought it with me."

"I wasn't planning on tonight."

"You have plans?"

She stared at the buttons on his red polo shirt. "No."

"Does Emily like picnics?"

After a quick appraisal down his navy casual slacks that registered neither approval nor disapproval, she said, "I thought we'd talk...alone."

"We can. But if we have a mouthful of potato salad we'll have less opportunity to be at each other's throats."

"Mr. Wescott..."

"And that has got to go. Jon. Try it. It's short for Jonathan."

She looked unsure, as if the situation were already beyond her control. Afraid she'd back out altogether, he encouraged, "C'mon. It's easier to say than Rumpelstiltskin."

She made the connection right away. "I wish there was a magic word to make this all go away."

"I know."

She tilted her head and searched his face. He felt uncomfortable, as if she could see far too much. Maybe even into the loneliness that made him want a relationship with his daughter.

Opening the screen door, she said, "All right...Jon. Come in."

She backed up so he didn't have to brush by her. Her expression said one false move and she'd not only call her lawyer but the police, too.

Alicia's living room was decorated in cool green and salmon. The ruffled curtains at the window matched the flowered slipcover on one of the chairs. The sofa was upholstered in the same green as the color in the curtains, another chair in the salmon. The occasional tables looked like antiques, but he couldn't be sure.

Shifting the parrot from the crook of his arm to his hand, he asked, "Think Emily will like it?"

"Presents aren't necessary."

"Maybe not for you." He could imagine what Alicia was thinking, that he wanted to be a type of Santa Claus to Emily to win her over. If presents would do it, he wasn't beyond buying them. And Alicia couldn't control what he gave his daughter.

Obviously realizing that, Alicia said, "She's in the kitchen. You're not going to tell her—"

"I won't say anything. Yet."

Alicia brushed her hair behind her ear. Adam Hobbs had not only confirmed Jon's information as accurate, but assured her that Jonathan Wescott was a prominent member of the community and a man of good character. But having Jon in her office was one thing; having him in her living room was another. She could only hope she was doing the right thing, for her and Emily.

Alicia had also called her lawyer and faxed him a copy of Cecile's letter. Because of the letter, along with Jon's willingness to take a paternity test, her attorney had urged her to try to keep relations with him civil. Being civil when she was scared to the tips of her toes that she could lose her daughter was a bit difficult. Besides the fact that he made all of her nerve endings stand on end. Whenever he got close, she . . . tingled.

Emily was happily pasting puffed popcorn kernels onto a piece of construction paper at the kitchen table. She looked up at her mother. "My tree's done. And I'm makin' a lamb— What's that?"

Jon set the bag on the table, then held out the parrot to Emily. "Like it?"

Her green eyes grew big. "Yeah!"

"It's yours."

"Really?" She checked with her mom. "Can I have it?"

Alicia saw it for the bribe it was. She also saw it as Jon's means of reaching out to a child he thought was his daughter. "Yes, you can. Would you like to have a picnic outside? Mr. Wescott brought supper."

"Roast beef sandwiches, potato salad, pickled eggs and chocolate éclairs."

Emily had wrinkled up her nose at the mention of roast beef. "What's a *ay-clir?*"

Alicia took the bag of popcorn and closed it with a twistie. "It's like a doughnut with pudding inside and chocolate icing on top." That brought a grin from the five-year-old. "But you have to eat some roast beef, too."

"Aw, Mom."

"What are you going to name your parrot?" Alicia asked.

"I don't know. I'll hafta think about it. Can I take him outside with us?"

"Sure. After you wash your hands." Emily patted the parrot, shoved it under her arm, and was about to run through the living room when Alicia reminded, "What do you say?"

The little girl turned to Jon and tilted her chin up. "Thank you."

The smile on his face lit up his eyes as he said, "You're very welcome."

Emily took off.

"Do you like iced tea? I made a pitcher this morning." As Alicia talked, she took paper plates from a cupboard. If she kept moving, maybe Jonathan Wescott wouldn't seem so...so...male.

"That's fine. Can I do anything to help?"

She grabbed a stack of napkins and took two glasses and a plastic cup from the cabinet above the dishwasher. "If you bring the food, I can get the rest."

At the table she put the plates and glasses on the bench. Spinning around, she said, "I forgot a tablecloth—" and bumped right into Jon.

Balancing the bag in one arm, his other went around her to steady her.

Lord, his chest was hard. All of him was hard. And he smelled like spice and male and... She had to get a grip. When she gazed up at him, the light in his green eyes scared her. It was intense and aware, and she knew he could see her pulse thudding at her throat. She took a step away, and his hand slid across her shoulders. Her mouth went dry and she stood immobilized.

He set the bag on the table. "Alicia, relax. I'm not going to steal your silverware, or Emily."

As his arm had gone around her, as his scent had made her dizzy, she hadn't been thinking about Emily. What was wrong with her? She didn't respond to men this way. Especially this kind of man with self-will, and self-confidence, and more male appeal than she knew how to categorize.

Not knowing what else to say, she murmured, "Excuse me," and went for the tablecloth.

Alicia and Emily went out to set the picnic table together. Jon followed and unpacked the supper while Alicia worked on half of one of the sandwiches, making it a size Emily could handle. Scooping out spoonfuls of the potato salad, Jon teased Emily about the size of her sandwich as compared to his.

"Are you married…Jon?" Alicia asked. Now why out of all the questions she could ask had she asked that one?

His half smile made her grip her fork a little tighter. "No. I never have been." As Emily's plate slid away from her, he pushed it closer and said, "Alicia, I really do need those programs and invitations we discussed. Can you tell the printer to go ahead with them?"

She shrugged. "Neither of us will turn away business."

"I wasn't so sure of that." His eyes met and held hers for a long moment. She broke contact and picked up her sandwich.

Her daughter chattered to Jon while they ate, telling him about her morning at school. He listened carefully, asking appropriate questions. At a lull in their conversation, he waved at the unfinished playhouse. "I bet you'd like to play in there when school's out."

Emily bobbed her head.

Finishing his sandwich, he scooped up a forkful of potato salad. "I'm pretty good with a hammer and nails."

Alicia protested, "I can't let you—"

"It would give me a chance to spend some time here."

He meant spend time with Emily. But then Alicia glanced at him and saw the sparks of interest in his eyes. She felt an answering spark inside her. Panic rose and she tamped it down. Without agreeing to his suggestion, she asked, "How long will you be in Camp Hill?"

"That depends on what happens."

"What about your business?"

"With fax machines and conference calls, I can handle most business from here."

In other words, she was stuck with him.

They finished eating, and started on dessert while a breeze began to blow. Emily thoroughly enjoyed her éclair, getting pudding around her mouth and chocolate icing on her nose. She giggled as Alicia wiped her face clean. "Can I go swing?" her daughter asked.

The sky had turned to a dark gray and a rumble of thunder vibrated across the yard. "For a few minutes. I think a storm's coming up."

Emily picked up her parrot and dashed toward the swings.

Jon laughed. "Does she ever walk?"

"Not if she can help it." An awkward silence settled over the table, made worse by the skittery feeling Jon's probing gaze caused Alicia.

"Tell me about you," Jon encouraged.

"There's not much to tell."

"I doubt that. Are you and Ria identical twins?"

"Yes."

"Obviously you're close."

"In each other's pockets, our teachers used to say."

"Any other brothers or sisters?"

"Nope. How about you?" Maybe if she could turn the attention on him, she wouldn't feel so stilted.

"An only child. My mother was always sorry about that."

"And what about you?"

"I would have liked a brother or sister to boss around, now and then."

She couldn't suppress a smile at his honesty. "Ria and I never bossed each other. We found out early that sticking together helped us both. When our father—" Stopping abruptly, she stacked the dirty plates in a pile. It wasn't like her to discuss her background.

"Problems in your childhood?"

"Most people have problems. You get through it. You go on."

"But not without repercussions."

He sounded as if he understood, as if he hadn't experienced the loving childhood she wanted so badly to give to her daughter.

Huge drops of rain began to splatter on the table. "Emily," she called. "Time to go in."

The rain didn't wait but fell from the clouds as if someone had turned over a giant sprinkling can. Alicia dumped the used paper goods into the now-empty deli bag. Jon grabbed the pitcher of tea and the glasses. Emily came running and they hurried inside.

Emily danced around the kitchen in a circle singing, "I got wet!"

Alicia dropped the bag into the trash. "Go dry off, honey."

As she turned, Jon opened the refrigerator and put the pitcher inside. He looked very at home in her kitchen. Grabbing a towel from the oven door handle, she swiped at her arms. Then she held it out to Jon. She couldn't help but notice the wet waving hair on his forearms.

His fingers covered hers. His hand was large, where hers was small. His was hot; hers was cool. The electricity of touching kept her from moving her hand or anything else. Jon Wescott was close and, good Lord, she wondered what his lips would feel like on hers.

He bent his head and then she didn't have to wonder anymore.

Chapter Three

Desire had gripped Jon before. But it had been a basic urge to satisfy, not an overwhelming need. This kind of need was new and foreign and arousing. His arms surrounded Alicia before he could think. His lips settled on hers, and with her gasp he slipped his tongue into her mouth. When he tasted her, every nerve in his body rejoiced and asked for more.

Until he realized she was stiff in his arms. What felt so right to him apparently did not feel right to her.

Alicia tried to concentrate. The shock of Jonathan Wescott's arms around her, the scorching heat of his kiss, the dizzying sensation of her mind whirling and her body aching, had frozen her into immobility. She'd never experienced anything like this with Patrick. Their embrace had always been a friendly give-and-take, not an assault on her senses, not fireworks, not so primal...

The voice of reason suddenly overcame Alicia's light-headedness and steadied the runaway speed of her pulse.

Was Jonathan Wescott coming on to her to get what he wanted? Did he think that since his offer of money didn't sway her, his sex appeal might? Did he believe that some…attraction would change how she felt about Emily? Or him?

Tearing away, she didn't know if she saw surprise in Jon's eyes or disappointment. Turning to the stove, she hung the towel over the oven's handle, trying to steady herself, trying to stop her body's trembling.

She knew all about men being nice when they wanted something. She and Ria had been around that behavior for years. Their father had rarely been nice to his wife. It wasn't until they were adults that the twins had figured out that he'd only been nice to their mother when he wanted sex. The rest of the time he'd treated her like a servant, and she'd let him.

Long ago Alicia had vowed no man would treat her that way, or control her, or direct her life. Patrick had been the epitome of gentleness and flexibility. They'd been considerate of each other's needs, and he'd never tried to bend her to his will. But this man…

"I'd better check on Emily," she murmured.

Jon wouldn't let her evade him that easily. When she turned around, he hadn't moved. "I think I misread the signals."

"I wasn't giving off any signals."

He studied her carefully. "I think you were. But something happened that you weren't ready for, didn't it?"

She didn't think she was ready for anything about Jonathan Wescott. He seemed to have a sensual power over her she didn't like at all. But she couldn't tell him that because it would put her at a disadvantage.

When she didn't answer his question, Jon said, "You're a beautiful woman, Alicia."

She felt her flush stain her cheeks. "And I have something you want."

"Meaning Emily?" he asked gently.

"What else would I mean?"

His brows hiked up. "Did you ever think that a man might want you for you?"

"But you're not just any man, are you? You think you're Emily's father. Of course I suspect ulterior motives."

He sighed. "You don't trust easily."

"I trust my sister and I trusted my husband. What grounds do I have to trust you?"

His tone was wry. "Score one for you. You're not as fragile as you look, are you?"

"Fragile? Take a better look, Mr. Wescott. You might see blond hair and blue eyes, but believe me, you will not see weakness."

He drew his hand dramatically across his forehead. "Whew. I asked for that one, didn't I? If I apologize, will you go back to calling me Jon?"

Ria often told her she was too touchy—around men. But this man made her feel vulnerable. She'd fought that feeling since childhood. "Are you apologizing?"

He smiled. "Yes. Are you accepting?"

She hesitated, yet couldn't help but return his smile. "Yes."

"Good. Because I'd like to come over tomorrow evening and work on the playhouse. It will give me a chance to be around Emily in a casual situation."

"And what if I don't think that's a good idea?"

"I'll find another way to see Emily with or without your approval."

Her choices were limited. She had no doubt he would follow his words with action. If she could somehow keep her distance, letting him work on the playhouse could be the lesser of all evils.

"Alicia, I won't kiss you again unless I know that's what you want, too."

Her dealings with Jon to this point had intimated that he was a man of his word. And if he was Emily's father, he and Emily could begin by building their relationship slowly. "If you want to work on the playhouse, go ahead."

As soon as she said the words, Jon's green eyes darkened with satisfaction, making her realize he'd won the battle if not the war.

Jon entered his suite feeling as if he'd just successfully negotiated a tough business deal. Alicia Fallon might have quiet beauty, she might be reserved and sometimes even seem shy, but she was no pushover. And damn it, he was attracted to her. Usually he didn't think twice about seeing what he wanted and grabbing it, or buying it, or negotiating for it. But when he kissed Alicia again, he wanted her to be willing and a full participant.

When? Not if? Jeez, he didn't need his life more complicated than it already was. Hadn't he decided after Cecile's departure from his life that a relationship with a woman was a bad investment? That the chance for substantial returns was too great a risk? For the past five years he'd engaged in low-risk, immediate-return encounters with women and invested his energy and time into adding to the Wescott holdings and making them successful.

Then, for some reason, he thought about Adam…and Jana—the woman who'd brought laughter and Adam's daughters back into his friend's life. They made marriage seem easy. But Adam and Jana were the exception.

As Jon took his wallet from his pocket and tossed it on the dresser, the phone rang. He picked it up automatically, used to receiving phone calls at all hours of the day or night.

"Mr. Wescott, it's Valerie Sentara. I understand you're looking into buying a newspaper in Harrisburg. Would you like to confirm or deny?"

Valerie Sentara wrote a gossip column for a newspaper in Los Angeles, one he didn't own, didn't hold shares of, or even consider a serious rival. She had a reputation for being ruthless in getting stories that would sell her publisher's papers. "Neither. What I'm doing here is nobody's business but mine. Go snooping somewhere else."

"But Mr. Wescott—"

"That's it, Ms. Sentara. No comment." Putting the receiver on its console, he realized he might have just stoked the reporter's curiosity. He'd have to make inquiries into newspapers in the area to cover his tracks. In no way did he want to thrust Alicia or Emily into the public eye. He'd protect them any way he could.

Before Jon had left Alicia's house Tuesday evening, she'd shown him the four foot by eight foot sheets of wood paneling in her garage intended for the inside of Emily's playhouse. So this afternoon, he'd gone to the lumberyard, purchasing two sawhorse kits, a circular saw, extension cord, hammer, nails, goggles and a trouble light. If he finished the interior first, Emily could play inside even if the shingles weren't yet attached to the roof.

He ate an early supper and arrived at Alicia's around five-thirty, wanting to take advantage of the light that was left. She came to the door with an apron covering her blouse and slacks. Red dots and one bright splash of tomato sauce stained the bib. He suddenly glimpsed a picture of coming home to a woman like this every night. It was more than palatable.

Without preamble and to avoid the awkwardness of small talk, he said, "I'll take the supplies around back. Do you have an outside electrical outlet, or do I need to plug into the house?"

Her gaze passed over his yellow T-shirt and denims, making him feel much hotter than the seventy degree weather called for. Women had looked at him before. In his position, he took that kind of attention for granted. But it was different with Alicia doing the looking than it had been with women in the past. He reminded himself, *You're not going to kiss her unless she wants you to.*

"There's an outlet on the back porch. Is there anything you need before you start?" Alicia asked.

"A glass of water would be nice. Other than that, I have everything I need. I hope."

"Have you done this type of thing before?"

"We had a handyman I followed around when I was a teenager. He taught me a little about plumbing, a little about construction." He'd been a friendly male influence when Jon's father was too busy to have anything to do with him.

Still staying behind the closed screen door, Alicia said, "We're just finishing supper. I'm sure Emily will want to watch you. Will it be safe?"

He wasn't surprised by Alicia's concern; he respected it. "I'll make it safe. Just send her out when she's finished supper."

As Jon carried supplies to the backyard, he felt Alicia's gaze on him more than once through the kitchen window. She was going to watch him like the proverbial hawk. He sighed. Somehow, he had to show her he only wanted to get to know his daughter.

The weather was comfortable until he started sawing and hammering, ducking in and out of the playhouse. Emily soon joined him with his glass of water, chattering away as he hammered. When he started the saw, Alicia appeared by her daughter's side, protectively holding her by the shoulders. He wanted to pretend her observant gaze didn't bother him, but the drops of sweat rolling down his neck came from more than exertion.

As he turned off the saw, Emily asked questions with the natural aptitude of children to absorb anything new that interested them. He couldn't help but wonder what her reaction would be if he told her he was her father.

Emily scooted over to her swing set. Jon took the sheet of paneling inside and was busily fitting it around the window, when, a few minutes later, Alicia stepped over the threshold. The scent of her perfume teased him. Lilacs. He'd smelled it the first time he'd stepped into her office, he'd noticed it again when they'd met at the Fourstar offices, he'd breathed it when he'd kissed her. It was very light, almost like a whiff on the breeze. Now it wrapped around him in the close quarters making his body respond in very real ways.

She offered him a tall tumbler. "I thought you might like some iced tea. Emily brought your empty water glass inside."

He grinned. "Mother's little helper?"

"Sometimes. But I don't want her to grow up too fast. I want her to run and play and just love being a child while she can."

Something in Alicia's voice told him she hadn't had that experience. He propped the paneling against the wall and took the tea from her hand. Two ice cubes bobbed near the top. Lifting the glass, he drank half of it in a few seconds.

He lifted it to her. "This is good. I've never tasted anything quite like it."

"I use orange juice instead of sugar."

"Health conscious?"

"Aware of what's good for Emily."

"You focus your entire life around her, don't you?"

Alicia shrugged. "I have my business. But she deserves my attention as well as my love."

"And you deserve a life. Have you dated since your husband died?"

She lifted her chin. "I came in to offer you something to drink, not to disclose my personal life."

Undaunted, he returned, "Do you have a personal life?"

Her mouth straightened into an angry line. "That's none of your business."

Leaning against the doorjamb, he took another swallow of tea. "Did I hit a nerve?"

Her gaze didn't seem to know where to settle. Finally he suspected it landed on his nose as she asked with annoyance, "Do you ever stop asking questions?"

"When I get answers."

"Then I guess you'll just have to keep asking questions. I put a dish of oatmeal cookies on the picnic table. I told Emily she had to leave you at least three."

"Did you make them?"

"Yes."

Jon grinned. "I haven't had homemade oatmeal cookies since I was a kid."

She hesitated a moment, then asked, "Do you live in Los Angeles?"

"I have a beach house in Malibu. It's worth the commute. I'd hate to be cooped up in an apartment."

Running her hand over the sheet of paneling he'd already attached, she asked, "Do you have much room at the hotel?"

"It's an efficiency suite." Her hand was small, delicate, smooth. He could imagine it... Blanking out the thought, he gestured to the playhouse. "But I get cabin fever easily and this project will get me out in the fresh air. You have a lot more of that here than we do in L.A."

Alicia took a step toward the door. "It'll be dark shortly. I'm going to take Emily inside and give her a bath."

"Can I tuck her in?"

"No," Alicia answered quickly. Then she added, "She's going to start asking questions."

"Don't friends of yours ever tuck her in?"

"Ria does and Gertie. And the baby-sitter I use sometimes. No one else."

"I think I just got the answer to my question." Before she could respond, he added, "What about reading Emily a story before bed? Certainly there's no harm in that."

Alicia weighed his suggestion, then answered, "All right. We'll be waiting in the living room."

He moved to the side so he wasn't blocking the door. "Alicia?"

She paused before ducking out.

"Thank you."

She nodded. He wondered if she knew he didn't mean for the iced tea but for letting him into their lives, however reluctantly.

Luckily he'd thrown a clean T-shirt into his car. After he'd stowed the sawhorses and supplies in Alicia's garage, he saw the spigot by the side of the house. He tugged his shirt over his head, turned the handle, took the end of the hose and stooped over, letting the water run over his neck.

Alicia heard the water go on as she dried off her daughter and helped her into her pajamas. Emily ran off to her room for a book, and Alicia peeped out the bathroom window. The last rays of light were slipping behind the tree line. Jon's profile was strong and clear as he wiped his face and neck with the T-shirt that had covered him earlier. When she'd taken him the iced tea, he'd been sweaty, the musky smell of hard work filling the playhouse. While he'd worked, his shirt had molded to his chest and his arms, delineating the muscle underneath. Obviously, he was not a man who spent all of his time in an office.

Now that he'd removed the shirt, Alicia could see his muscles rippling. She was enthralled by the shadows playing over his back and wondered how much hair he had on his chest. She'd seen the dark curls peeping over the crew neck of his shirt.

Without warning, Jon turned around and she got a good look at the dark curling hair dividing his chest, swirling around his nipples, and whorling under his belt buckle. Her breath stuck in her throat . . . until he looked up and saw her watching. Suddenly she thought she'd never breathe again. Male-female awareness. Stark. Intense. Frightening.

Turning away from the window, she braced her arms on the sink. She ran the cold water and splashed her cheeks, then took a deep breath and wiped them, knowing the best thing for her to do was to get Jon Wescott out of her house the minute her daughter went to bed.

Jon's baritone was hypnotic as he read Emily a story about a little engine who wouldn't give up. The sound of his voice rose and fell and changed tone. He related to her daughter so easily, Alicia thought. And Emily apparently liked him. With some people she'd shyly back off. But she hadn't done that with Jon. Right now, cuddled in the crook of his arm, she couldn't look any more comfortable or contented.

Jon made no move to leave after he finished the story. As Emily waved good-night and took Alicia's hand, he crossed his ankle over his knee and said, "I'll wait until you put Emily to bed."

Emily tugged on her mother's hand and stopped abruptly on the first step. "Mr. Wescott, can you come to carnival day on Saturday?"

He looked to Alicia for an explanation.

"Our church has a bazaar on Saturday. A penny carnival, bingo, turkey dinner in the evening." Her attitude suggested it was nothing he'd enjoy.

"It's fun," Emily insisted. "Can you come? Mommy's gonna work at the flower stand."

"Only for two hours before dinner," Alicia added.

"Who's going to watch Emily?"

Already he sounded like a parent. "Ria will stop in for a while."

"She throws pennies real good," Emily informed him. "Do you?"

"I can't remember the last time I threw pennies. You might have to show me how."

"You'll come?" Emily asked eagerly.

Jon smiled. "Sure."

Sure, Alicia repeated to herself as she walked with Emily up the stairs. The man was invading every inch of her life and enjoying himself while he did it. It frightened her. What if Emily not only got to know Jon, but got attached? What if Jonathan Wescott was being agreeable now only to try to take Emily away later? What was the best thing to do? Push him away? Then would he take her to court? All she could do was take one day at a time, hoping she made the right choices.

Jon was still sitting on the sofa when she returned. "I'll need directions," he said easily.

"You don't have to come. If you feel roped into this..."

"I've never been to a church bazaar."

Her brows arched. "Never?"

"Nope. My mother has served on charity boards, but we never belonged to a church."

Alicia lighted on the edge of the chair near the sofa. "I can't imagine that. My mother took Ria and me every Sunday. It was routine, part of what we did. After Patrick died, it became more than a routine, and I guess I realized why she'd done it all those years."

"Why?"

Questions again. Was Wescott Industries a think tank? Alicia couldn't see the harm in answering him this time. "She found comfort there she couldn't find anywhere else."

"Did you find comfort there?" he asked, his green eyes sympathetic.

She couldn't help but respond to the caring in his voice. "Thank God, I wasn't alone like my mother. I had Ria. But, yes, I found comfort there."

"Your father is dead?"

"Yes. But my mother felt alone all through her marriage. Church was the one place she could escape to without him going on a rampage." Alicia could see more questions in Jon's eyes, questions she didn't want to answer. Again, she'd revealed too much. What about this man made her do that?

Jon surprised her by giving a bit of his own history. "My father died shortly after Cecile left Los Angeles. Even though she'd ended the relationship, I probably would have tried to contact her, but suddenly I had my responsibilities *and* my father's, too. My mother has an accountant, but she'd never been involved in the business. I didn't realize until after Dad was gone how much she'd leaned on him."

"Did they have a good marriage?" Alicia knew her background had affected her view of relationships. Had Jon's?

He cocked his head and seemed to look into the past. "To tell the truth, I'm not sure. Dad worked constantly. Mom had her own interests. I saw little affection between them. Yet, they had this bond I could feel when I was around them. One of mutual respect and deep commitment."

"Mutual respect. That's what I never saw between my parents," Alicia murmured.

Focusing on her again, his gaze lingered on her lips. "Where's your mother now?"

Alicia took in a quick breath. "She lives with her sister in Ohio."

Jon put his feet flat on the floor and shifted toward her. "Wouldn't she rather be near her daughters and her granddaughter?"

Her heart always hurt when she thought of her mother. "As a companion for Aunt Edna, she doesn't have to pay rent or many other expenses. She's never held a full-time job or been on her own. After my father died, she didn't know where to start. This was the easy way out for her."

"Then you don't see her often?"

Alicia brushed her thumb back and forth across the arm of her chair. "Ria and I try to drive out three or four times a year. But we have to make all the effort."

"If my mother knew about Emily, she'd visit as often as she could. She loves kids. Most of the charity work she does is for children's organizations."

Alicia thought about Emily having another grandmother, another family. "Who does know, Jon?"

"Adam, my lawyer in Los Angeles. And the lawyer I retained here." He leaned forward. "Will you have dinner with me tomorrow night?"

"Why?" she asked, unable to keep the wariness from her voice.

"Because I enjoy talking to you. And because a friendship between us will help where Emily's concerned."

A friendship. Is that what Jonathan Wescott really wanted? Maybe she'd mistaken the intensity of his kiss, the look in his eyes earlier, the heat between them. Maybe she was overreacting to the whole situation. But the fear of losing Emily had been a weight on her heart since Jon had announced he was her father. If she found out more about him, maybe he wouldn't seem so threatening. And maybe she'd have ammunition if she needed it.

"If Ria can't stay with Emily, I can probably get a baby-sitter. If there's a problem, I'll call you."

When he stood, so did she. He walked to the door and she followed. Instead of opening the screen door, though, he turned toward her. She got caught in the green of his eyes. The heat began again and her heart raced.

He gently brushed her cheek with his thumb. "I'm looking forward to tomorrow night. I'll pick you up at seven."

If she moved, she'd break the spell. If she moved, she knew he'd kiss her. She stood perfectly still.

He dropped his hand and opened the screen door. As she heard his car start, she sagged against the wall. He might say he wanted friendship, but she guessed he wanted more. How much more?

Alicia was furious, absolutely furious. Thursday afternoon, gripping a letter she'd received in the mail, she lifted the phone and dialed. When Jon picked up at his end, she slapped the letter down on her blotter. "Exactly what type of visitation rights do you intend to file for, Mr. Wescott? You want friendship? I don't think so. Friendship requires trust. How can I trust you when you go behind my back?"

He swore, the kind of words her father used to use. Alicia almost hung up. But she'd never stood up to her father, and she was going to stand up to Jonathan Wescott. "I don't deserve that kind of—"

"No, you don't. Alicia, I told Adam to draw up the papers when I first found out about Emily. Truthfully, I'd forgotten about them."

"Forgotten you want visitation rights?"

"Of course not. Forgotten I'd asked Adam to send them. Then, I thought I was going to have to fight you every step of the way."

"You are. I'll have my lawyer call you. There's no proof you're Emily's father and if you think I'm going to sign away rights without any proof, you're mistaken."

"Be reasonable, Alicia. Let's talk about it at dinner tonight."

"Dinner? Dinner's off. I can't be friends with someone I can't trust."

"Don't do this, Alicia. I'll file for more than visitation rights if you don't give me access to Emily. I'll get a court order for the paternity testing and sue for custody."

"You just try it," she retorted, her voice strained as she tasted the bitterness of fear and held back her tears. Hanging up, Alicia not only felt afraid and angry, but she also felt a sorrow that didn't belong. Why? Because she was beginning to like Jonathan Wescott? Because she was attracted to him in a way she'd never been attracted to another man?

None of that mattered now because she was in for the fight of her life.

Jon slammed down the receiver, angry with himself. He was slipping. He'd forgotten he'd told Adam to send the damn letter. So now Alicia thought he'd been manipulating her.

He shouldn't have threatened her. But it wasn't in his nature to back down or to give up easily. He couldn't give up on his daughter... or Alicia. There was only one thing to do—confront her openly and make her see his point of view.

Saturday afternoon, he found the only church in Alicia's area of Camp Hill having a bazaar. The sun shone on the parking lot and the wooden stands, some covered with canopies. The spring breeze ruffled his hair and flipped the collar of his blue polo shirt. He didn't care. He was only concerned with finding Alicia and convincing her... What? That he wasn't a calculating, ruthless scoundrel? He felt like a scoundrel when he was with her. He wanted to carry her off somewhere, kiss her senseless... Damn. When had his interest shifted to Alicia?

He still wanted to be a father to his daughter, get to know her. But he wanted to spend a lot more time with Alicia, too. Why? So they could have a torrid affair? That could harm his chances of getting joint custody of Emily more than help them. Because when affairs were over...

He finally caught sight of Alicia. She was standing among a backdrop of flowers. Bunches of lilacs stood in a bucket in one corner. Hyacinths, mums and daisies lined the waist-high shelf. In back of her, dried flower arrangements hung in bouquets, on fans, with lace and ribbons. She was smiling at a woman who'd bought a pot of mums.

Alicia's lavender blouse with its demure yet alluring boat neckline, her lavender slacks and white espadrilles, made her look like a spring vision. He just hoped she wouldn't turn into a summer storm when she saw him. At least in a public place she wasn't likely to call the police. Or make a scene. A woman like Alicia would hate making a scene.

He waited until the lady with the mums strolled away, then he walked to the stand and plucked one lilac from the bunch. Alicia was facing the cash box and didn't notice him. He tapped her on the shoulder with the lilac.

Her expression was priceless—shock, surprise and a moment later a whole lot of anger.

He held out the lilac to her. "I thought here you wouldn't call for reinforcements."

"Well, you thought wrong." She stepped out from behind the makeshift counter and scanned the crowd.

"You can't leave the stand unattended. You'll lose sales."

She looked at the cash box and the flowers that were left. Then she faced him squarely. "I don't want to talk to you."

"I know you don't. But I want to talk to you."

"Why? So you can charm me, and persuade me, and pull the wool over my eyes again?"

"No."

Not seeing whoever she was trying to find in the crowd, she stepped behind the counter again. It was a tangible barrier between them.

Laying the lilac down in front of her, he decided he'd buy out all the flowers at the stand if he thought it would help. A realization came swiftly like a bolt of lightning—Alicia couldn't be bought. He suddenly knew that as well as his own name. So what would it take to get her to listen to him?

The unvarnished truth.

Holding her gaze, he said, "After our first meeting, I told Adam to send you the letter. I didn't think I had a choice. After our meeting in your sister's office, I was sure of it. But then you agreed to let me into your life, and I forgot about it. All I had on my mind was getting to know Emily."

He saw the wariness in Alicia's eyes, and he didn't blame her. No one liked to be taken advantage of. That was exactly what she'd thought he'd done.

She braced her hands on the wooden counter as if bracing herself for a blow. "Are you going to file for visitation rights? Custody?"

"I'm not going to string you along, Alicia. I want to have the paternity testing done. I think you need to know for sure that I'm Emily's father. Living with uncertainty is more difficult than facing the truth."

"I don't know," she said quietly.

He covered one of her hands with his. "I'm not going to go away." All at once he realized that even if Emily weren't involved, he'd want to get closer to this complex woman who backed off whenever he got too close.

"Mr. Wescott, Mr. Wescott. You came! I want to win a goldfish but I can't throw the ball into the bowl. Can you do it?"

Emily let go of Ria's hand and ran toward him, waiting for his answer.

He saw the message Ria exchanged with Alicia with her eyes. It was a "do-you-need-help-dealing-with-him?" look. His usual confrontational tactics that had worked well in his past, obviously didn't work with Alicia Fallon. There was a delicate balance at stake here, a matter of her beginning to trust him. She might if he put some of the control in her hands. It was worth a shot.

He crouched down to Emily's level. "I can try to win you a goldfish. But your mom might have other plans."

"Mommy?"

Alicia studied Jon stooped down with her daughter. She met his gaze and seemed to try to see into his soul. Maybe she did because she asked him, "Do you like turkey and stuffing?"

"I haven't had it since Thanksgiving. I'm due."

"Then, see if you can win this lovely child a goldfish and afterward we'll go have something to eat. My replacement is due any minute."

The muscles in his shoulders relaxed. Standing, he let his daughter pull him toward the goldfish stand only a few feet away.

Alicia hoped she wasn't making a mistake. She didn't trust easily. But something about Jon led her to trust him. Maybe it was the way he laid everything out on the table. He didn't sugarcoat it, and he spoke plainly. He had an agenda of his own, and he pushed to get it accomplished. In some ways, Jon Wescott reminded her of her father. Yet in others . . .

Her father had been overbearing, never listening to the people around him. Jon, on the other hand, seemed to listen.

"What are you going to do?" Ria asked her as she watched Jon toss his first ball.

"I'm not sure. If he is her father, I have to let him into her life. For her sake. We never felt dad's love, or had his affection. If Emily has a chance to know a father's love, I can't take that away from her, no matter how the circumstances might affect me." After a moment of silence, she nodded toward her daughter and said softly, "She likes him."

"Do you?" her twin asked.

"I haven't thought about it."

Ria shook her head. "Liar. He's one attractive specimen."

"We both know that doesn't mean anything."

Since her last relationship, Ria had as much trouble trusting as Alicia. Tugging down her fringed, multicolored vest, her twin agreed, "That's for sure. Do you want me to stick around?"

Alicia again glanced toward Jon and Emily. How could she be attracted to a man who might be able to take her daughter away? It didn't make sense. But Jon Wescott was *her* problem, not Ria's. "No. There's no reason for you to stay." She forced a smile. "I know you're meeting friends for supper. Go have fun."

"You're sure?"

Alicia nodded.

Ria stuffed her hands into her pockets. "You call me if you need me. I won't be out late."

"We'll be okay."

Ria glanced over at Jon's broad shoulders as he tossed a Ping-Pong ball into a fishbowl and Emily cheered. Murmuring, "Maybe you will," she gave Alicia a hug and left the parking lot.

A few minutes later, Alicia's replacement took over the flowers. Gertie Abbott, who was tending another of the craft stands, agreed to watch Emily's new goldfish while she, Jon and Alicia ate dinner. Emily led Jon and her mother into the all-purpose room, picking up her tray and methodically placing a spoon, fork and napkin on the plastic surface.

Jon's shoulder brushed Alicia's as he said, "I can't remember the last time I went through a cafeteria line."

Trying to alleviate the tension between them, she asked lightly, "They don't have cafeterias in Los Angeles?"

He gave her a crooked smile. "I'll have to check."

His smile caused almost as much turmoil as the set of his jaw when he was confronting her about Emily. Alicia moved her tray down the row next to her daughter's. "Exactly what is Wescott Industries? Do you manufacture something?"

"No." His face became serious. "It's the parent company. We're involved in many business ventures but our main concern is newspapers."

"You own them?"

"Yes."

She'd guessed Jon was wealthy from the easy way he'd offered her money. He'd just confirmed the fact.

"What's wrong?" he asked, seeing her frown.

"You wouldn't have a problem funding a court battle."

"No, I wouldn't." He picked up a pint-size carton of milk.

Emily saw friends from her kindergarten class and asked if she could sit with them. Alicia gave her okay and she and Jon chose an empty table where they could still see Emily.

Jon pushed Alicia's chair in for her and sat facing her. "Emily's a well-adjusted child, isn't she?"

"I hope so."

Then with the unflinching candor she was coming to expect from him, Jon asked, "Will you agree to the paternity testing?"

Alicia knew she had reached a moment of truth. How she answered would affect the rest of their lives—hers, Emily's and Jon's.

Chapter Four

Alicia studied her silverware for a moment, then looked up into Jon's waiting green eyes. "I need to know for sure and so do you. I'll call Emily's pediatrician Monday morning."

Jon reached over and covered her hand with his. "You're making the right decision."

She tried to resist the pull of Jon's appeal, the warmth of his palm, the sincerity on his face. "I'm doing it for Emily. She deserves to know her father, especially if he wants to be a part of her life." The small element of uncertainty helped her to keep the situation less personal.

Jon, of course, sensed what she was doing. He pulled back his hand. "I understand the results take about six weeks. I suppose it depends on the lab's backlog. My lawyer will try to keep the wait shorter, rather than longer."

"For an extra fee?" she guessed.

He shrugged. "If that's what it takes. Don't worry about it. I want the testing. I'll pay for it. When do you think Emily's doctor can fit us in?"

Her consent to the testing had just put the ball in motion. Jon's determination would keep it speeding ahead. "He has office hours all day Monday. Maybe we could go in before Emily's swimming lessons. She looks forward to them and won't think about the visit to the doctor's so much."

"Where does she take lessons?"

"The Y."

"I'd like to come along and watch."

It wasn't a request, but not quite a demand, either. If Jon was Emily's father, she'd have to be careful that he didn't dominate their lives. She wouldn't let that happen. She wouldn't let his wishes always override theirs.

"Alicia, you have to understand that I've missed five years of her life. I don't want to miss any more."

She couldn't fight with that reasoning or the sadness behind his words. Wishing she didn't understand his motives, wishing she didn't empathize with him, wishing she wasn't attracted to him, Alicia started on her turkey dinner with no appetite and with the fear that her life would never be the same again.

Holding a clipboard, the white-haired doctor peered over his wire-rimmed spectacles at Alicia and Jon while Emily played with toys in the waiting area. "Your lawyer faxed a list of instructions, Mr. Wescott. I understand a courier is waiting to drive the samples to Pittsburgh?"

Jon nodded. "That's correct. Proper labeling and handling is essential."

Jon had told Alicia she'd have to provide pictures of herself and Emily, as well as let the nurse take their fingerprints. Apparently the lawyer's instructions were very specific.

The doctor frowned. "I'm familiar with the procedures. I told your lawyer I don't do this every day, but more often than you'd think. That's why I have an inked pad for taking fingerprints."

Alicia nervously rubbed her arms, trying to ignore Jon's presence beside her, his defined muscles, the curling hair on his forearms. He looked composed and relaxed in his yellow polo shirt and forest green slacks. She wished she could calm her insides. "Dr. Thatcher, how accurate is this test?"

He set the clipboard on the counter attached to the examining room wall. "With all three blood samples, its accuracy rate can be near 99.9 percent if the analysis is taken that far."

His one phrase caught her attention. "All *three?*"

Dr. Thatcher looked down at his notes. "Yes, as I understood Mr. Wescott's lawyer, the lab already has Miss Braddock's blood samples in storage."

Alicia's heart pounded as she swung around to Jon. "You didn't tell me that. How is it possible?"

Jon leaned forward, closer to her, and she knew he meant the gesture to be comforting. "Before Cecile died, she sent the samples to the lab for this purpose."

Alicia felt threatened rather than comforted, and the magnitude of his statement hit her with imposing force. "So she was as sure as you are."

His gaze held hers. "Yes. But you have to be sure, too. That's why we're here."

She also heard what Jon wasn't saying. If he took her to court, he needed the documented proof. She might as well accept the inevitable—it looked as if Jon Wescott would be a permanent presence in their lives. If she didn't want to hurt her daughter, she should facilitate his visits with Emily so she could get used to him.

Alicia filled out and signed the appropriate forms, then went to the waiting room for Emily. She'd explained to her daughter exactly what the doctor would do, that this was a special test to see if her blood looked like Jon's. Emily volunteered to go first. Alicia noticed that already her daughter did and said things to get Jon's approval. At the carnival as they'd played bingo, she'd tried to keep all her markers in neat rows. This afternoon, when he'd come to pick them up, she'd asked if he'd like some iced tea. Did she need a male role model in her life so desperately?

Alicia remembered trying to earn her father's approval. Over and over. Ria had given up trying long before he died. But even to the last, Alicia had tried to be quiet enough, pretty enough, talented enough, to win words of encouragement. They'd never come.

She looked over at Jon again. He related so well to Emily. He talked to her on her level. He praised her. Would it be so difficult to accept him as her father? What was more difficult was accepting his masculine dominance, his ideas, and the obvious effect he had on her nervous system.

Luckily they finished at the doctor's office in plenty of time to reach Emily's lesson. Alicia directed Jon to the bleachers in the pool area while she took her daughter into the women's locker room.

Jon watched as Emily joined her class at the edge of the Olympic-size pool and waved to him. Alicia climbed to the third bench of the bleachers and sat next to him, careful not to let her arm brush his. She straightened her shoulders and propped her feet on the bench below her.

He didn't know how to break through Alicia's barriers. Just when he thought he'd made some progress...

The steamy humidity of the pool area brought out the flowery essence of Alicia's perfume. She'd worn pink slacks again today and a white knit top trimmed in the same color. The colors she wore suited her quiet beauty.

Jon caught her take a quick glance at him. Was she as aware of him as he was of her? He'd seen the trapped look in her eyes at the doctor's office when she'd learned about Cecile's blood sample, and he was sure she was feeling backed into a corner. But she had to get used to the reality. He was going to be a part of their lives.

His heart lodged in his throat when Emily jumped into the water. "Isn't that too deep for her? It's practically up to her neck!"

"She knows how to swim," Alicia responded quietly.

"She's only five."

"And I've been bringing her to this program for two years. She loves the water, Jon. The instructor is right there. She's not in any danger."

"Two years?"

"They start early now."

"I'll say," he muttered. "I couldn't tie my shoes at her age."

"I've heard boys are a little slower than girls."

When he turned his head, he saw the amusement in her eyes and the smile she was holding in check. "In some areas."

She let the smile break loose.

It dazzled him. "You are really beautiful when you smile."

The smile disappeared and her expression grew wary.

"What's wrong? Do you think I'm feeding you a line?" Her high color indicated her embarrassment, and he knew he'd hit the mark.

"You want something, and I think you might do anything necessary to get it."

Firmly planting his feet on the bleachers under him, he said, "Look, Alicia. I've been honest with you. And I intend to stay honest with you. It's not going to help my cause or my relationship with Emily if I try to take any shortcuts. If I say you're beautiful, it's because I mean it. No other reason."

She looked down into her lap.

"Alicia?" When she lifted her gaze to his, he saw the confusion. "Who made you so distrustful? Your husband?"

"No. Patrick never lied to me. He never tried to trade favors."

That was an unusual phrase for her to use. "Trade favors?"

"Never mind." She looked at Emily as she kicked up the swimming lane with an orange kickboard.

Jon had to touch Alicia. He had to find out more about this complicated lady. Laying his hand on her arm, he said, "Alicia, I want to mind. Let me know a little more about you."

"I told you more about me the other night than I tell most people."

He remembered their discussion about their mothers. "Tell me more." She shifted uncomfortably, and he slid his hand down her arm and covered her hand on the bench. He felt her tremble, and her response to his touch made his blood run faster.

Staring straight ahead, she curled her fingers under his but didn't move away. "My dad wanted boys. I don't think he knew how to relate to girls. When he wasn't working on a construction site, he watched television and drank beer. He always treated Mom like a slave, and she let him. But when he wanted something only she could give him, he could be very sweet. It was the only time."

Alicia had been afraid of her father, that was obvious. Is that why she'd married an older man, as a substitute for the father who'd never treated her as a daughter? That wouldn't be so surprising.

Jon ran his thumb across her knuckles. "You can trust me, Alicia."

"I don't know that yet," she said softly.

"You will," he murmured.

Her wide blue eyes met his. There were questions there, and doubts, and more than enough fear.

Slowly he'd clear all of that away. "Will you and Emily have dinner with me when we're finished here? I don't know the area so you'll have to choose someplace she'd like to go."

Alicia only hesitated a moment. "There's a strip shopping center not too far away that has a family restaurant. They have the best broasted chicken in the area. Emily loves it."

"It sounds good to me."

"It's just an ordinary restaurant, nothing fancy...."

"We don't need fancy, do we?" If anybody had told him two weeks ago he'd be sitting in a Y and looking forward to eating in a less than five-star restaurant, he would have told them they were crazy.

She smiled and answered him. "Maybe we don't."

He suddenly realized eating at a hot dog stand with Alicia could top any five-star restaurant on his list.

Alicia helped Emily start the zipper on her flannel jacket, then zipped up her own against the cooler evening air. As Jon walked with them under the canopy of the shopping center past a row of shops, he tried to sort his thoughts. He hadn't had a fountain milkshake since he was a teenager. He hadn't enjoyed a restaurant meal so much in years. Emily had talked nonstop throughout the meal, spreading her napkins one after the other across the table and over her lap. When she'd spilled her water, Alicia hadn't scolded but had signalled the waitress and encouraged Emily to help her mop up the water with fresh napkins. The quiet conversation he'd enjoyed with Alicia about her professional background while Emily concentrated on a chicken leg had been comfortable and more than pleasant. He couldn't remember when he'd enjoyed a conversation with a woman more, or being with a woman more.

Why? Because she was Emily's mother? No. Because she was a lady with a lot of class. A lady who awakened basic instincts. A lady who could cause more than a few complications in his life. Five years ago he'd decided he didn't need a relationship with a woman for anything beyond the physical wants of both parties. But Alicia Fallon was making him reexamine his thinking; that in itself was unsettling him.

Suddenly Emily skipped in front of him and pointed to something in the window. "Look, Mommy. There's that vase you like."

Jon stooped down beside Emily as she pressed her nose against the glass. The object in her sight was an iridescent vase about nine inches tall. He glanced at Alicia. "Do you want to go in and look at it?"

Emily piped up. "We always do."

He stood, took Emily's hand and opened the door for Alicia. She preceded him inside.

The shop displayed a selection of collectibles. Some of them looked very old, and Jon realized it was an antique shop. Alicia picked up the vase, her thumb ridging the flower pattern.

"Didn't I see dishes like that in your hutch?"

"Yes. I've been collecting for years. I now have four cups and saucers and five luncheon plates. But I find mine at yard sales and flea markets."

His fingers grazed hers as he took the vase from her. The warmth of her skin tingled on his fingertips as he turned it upside down and glimpsed the price. It wouldn't make a dent in his wallet, but he guessed it would in hers.

"Are there many of these around?"

"Some patterns in this type of glassware are easier to find than others. All of it is becoming more rare. Families are holding onto it. As you can see, this one's in perfect condition, that's why the price is so high. So I'll just keep looking. You'd be surprised how the price goes down with one little chip."

He didn't want her to have a chipped vase, but a perfect one. Gently he set the vase on the shelf.

Jon drove back to Alicia's, insisting on walking them to the door. Emily scurried inside then ran back to Jon. "Are you gonna read me a story?"

"I'd like to, honey. But I have to get back to the hotel. I'm expecting some phone calls. Maybe tomorrow. I'll come over tomorrow night and work on the playhouse."

"Okay. See ya." She was off in a flash.

"I hope tomorrow night's all right," he said, for the first time in a long time considering someone's schedule besides his own. He was entranced by the way Alicia's lovely blond hair spilled over her forehead and waved gently around her face.

"It's fine. We don't have any plans. Gertie's away this week, so I'll probably be doing laundry tomorrow night."

"If she's away, who's taking care of Emily?"

"I am. Gertie and her husband went to Williamsburg this week because I'm caught up. I have orders coming in, but not many appointments. Emily can color or play with her blocks while I work on a few design projects."

More and more he admired Alicia and the way she handled her life. "You have it all under control, don't you?"

She smiled. "I try."

That smile of hers did the strangest things to him. It made him feel younger and more alive, as if dreams were still possible. He'd wanted to touch her hair since the first day he'd met her. Taking a lock, he savored its silkiness. "I enjoyed today, Alicia."

The pulse at her throat fluttered rapidly. "Dinner was nice. I forget I need to socialize with adults."

He brushed her cheek with his thumb. "You haven't lost your touch."

"Ria keeps me on my toes." She sounded as breathless as he felt.

As he stroked her cheekbone, he moved in closer. The last time he'd kissed her with sudden hunger, searching for immediate satisfaction. But here, with her now, knowing some of her background, he realized more was at stake than momentary gratification. Bending to her, he touched her lips with his in a kiss filled with a gentleness of which he'd never known he was capable. Alicia stood perfectly still when he pressed his mouth against hers, then moved back and forth slowly in a brushing caress.

Restraining the surge of need that rushed through him, calling on the self-discipline he'd honed through adulthood, he backed away and fought the urge to draw her tight into his arms.

She looked a bit dazed.

He felt dazed, too. He'd never realized gentleness could be erotic. So erotic, he'd better leave *now*. "I'll see you tomorrow."

She nodded.

He remembered the stars in her blue eyes all the way to the hotel. As he undressed for bed, he could only think of their next kiss, of discovering more of everything about Alicia Fallon.

When Alicia awakened the next morning, she knew something was different. The sky had fallen in with Jon's kiss. This one hadn't even been a "real" kiss and it had heated her and shaken her for the rest of the evening. When he'd said good-night, his voice had been husky. Had the kiss shaken him, too?

Probably not. Not a man of his experience.

Alicia couldn't put Jon or the kiss out of her thoughts as she dressed, looked in on Emily who was still sleeping and went downstairs. Mixing pancake batter, she realized her guard had slipped last night, and she didn't know if that was good or bad. Jon's powerful masculinity still scared her. So did his determination and confidence.

The phone rang and her heart did a hopeful little flip. But it wasn't Jon. It was a crisis.

At noon Jon rang Alicia's office doorbell. He told himself he just wanted to tell her he would pick up Chinese or something for dinner. He'd tried to call, but he couldn't get through. Besides, he didn't want to wait until tonight to see her again. He'd called himself an idiot at least ten times for giving in to the impulse to drop by, but impulses had paid off in the past in business. Maybe it was time he should be more impulsive in his personal life.

Trying the door, he found it open. He walked in and saw an office that was not as organized as the last time he'd seen it. The computer blinked at him. Copies of some kind of design lay in disarray across the desk. Half a glass of milk sat on top of the papers, precariously close to the edge.

He went to the bottom of the steps and heard clattering and the hum of Alicia's voice. "Alicia?" he called, not wanting to startle her by suddenly appearing.

"Up here," she called back.

He climbed the steps, stopping at the top at the sight that greeted him. Alicia held the phone hugged between her ear and shoulder while she tried to cut a sandwich in half. The counter was littered with pancakes on a plate, batter in a bowl and an open carton of milk. All of it looked like the remains from breakfast because she had packages of ham and cheese in front of her now. Dirty dishes tilted over in the sink.

Emily sat at the table with a coloring book. She glanced up at Jon. "Mommy's busy."

"Busy" didn't quite cut it, and he wondered what had happened. He openly listened to Alicia's phone conversation. "I'll try to have a couple of designs ready, though it might be late." She stopped for a moment to listen. "All right. I'll finish them by tonight and fax them to your home. You choose the one you want and then call me. I have to get your choice into the computer and then shoot it. Doug said he'll be on stand-by for tomorrow and can probably fit in the business cards and pamphlets late in the day. We should have them for Friday."

She dropped the knife in the sink and reached for the cupboard that held glasses. "I'll call you first thing in the morning to tell you for sure." She listened for another moment, said, "I'll try," and hung up.

Seeing Jon, she blew out a breath and put Emily's sandwich on the table in front of her. Alicia's gaze hadn't quite met his, and he wondered if she felt shy because of their good-night kiss the evening before.

"What's wrong?" he asked, intuitively knowing Alicia would never have let him see her or her house in this condition if she'd had a choice.

"Jon, I don't want to be rude, but my day is totally out of hand. If you came to visit—"

"I came to ask you what I should bring for dinner."

That made her pause for a moment. "I'm probably not going to have time for dinner. I haven't had a chance yet to call Ria and see if she'll take Emily somewhere. With my luck today, she'll be working late." She poured Emily a glass of milk and set it on the table. The next minute she'd ducked into the refrigerator and searched the shelves. Finding a plastic bag filled with carrots and celery, she set it beside her daughter's plate.

He leaned against the counter. "So why won't you have time for dinner? I thought you were caught up."

"Because I designed a logo for a new sports supplies store. I used a football and baseball and basketball because that's what the owner wanted. He just found out another company has a similar logo. He wants a new one."

Jon knew the intricacies of dealing with everyone from advertisers to CEO's. "Is that a problem?"

Her hands fluttered before she picked up the strips of cheese on the cutting board and set them on Emily's plate. "It wouldn't be. But the store opens Friday and he needs the business cards and brochures to hand out. I have to redo everything.''

''I hope he's paying you well for this.''

''At this point, money's not the problem. I'm afraid my muse won't work well on a time limit. What if I can't produce something he likes?''

''You know you can,'' Jon said quietly, taking a long look at her disarrayed hair she'd brushed off her forehead, her jeans and faded blue T-shirt with Hersheypark emblazoned on the front. She was sexy as hell when ruffled.

Shoving the milk into the refrigerator, she closed the door with her elbow. ''Jon, it's not that simple. I need to concentrate. I've been at it for the past two hours and I don't like anything I've done. It's not unique enough. And this time, unique is what he wants.''

''Are there any playgrounds around here?''

She looked as if she couldn't possibly have heard him correctly. ''Playgrounds?''

He pushed away from the counter. ''Yeah. After Emily finishes lunch, she and I could go swing and slide.'' He winked at the little girl. ''Playground equipment should be able to hold me.''

''Oh, Mommy, can I go?'' Mayonnaise on her upper lip, she swiveled around to Jon. ''Can we ride on the seesaw, too?''

''If they have one.''

''I can't ask you to—''

''Spend some time with my...with Emily?'' Jon asked her, catching himself. ''It's a beautiful day out there. We'll have a blast. And that way, you can work uninterrupted.''

Alicia bit her lower lip. Jon had noticed it was a mannerism she used whenever she was undecided.

Emily hopped off her chair and went to her mother. "I promise if we have broccoli tonight, I'll eat all of it."

Alicia laughed and stooped down to hug her daughter. "All right. A couple of hours would really help. And if Ria can come over later—"

"I can take Emily somewhere for supper or bring something in. Don't bother Ria."

Alicia straightened. "I don't want to take advantage of you."

"I want to do this, Alicia. I was going to be here working on the playhouse anyway."

Emily ran back to the table and stuffed the last corner of her sandwich into her mouth and took a swallow of milk. "I'm ready. Can we go now?"

Alicia seemed to list the pros and cons in her mind. He knew *he* was the one taking advantage of the situation, and she knew it, too. But she must have decided in his favor because she asked Emily, "Can you show J . . . Mr. Wescott how to get there?"

"Sure." She grabbed his hand. "Let's go out the front door. It's closer."

He shrugged. "That settles it. We'll be back sometime." He added, "And don't worry. I'll take good care of her." Alicia's worried frown made him realize she still didn't trust him with Emily. He'd prove she could.

At first, Alicia checked her watch every ten minutes. Finally she told herself she had to relax and give Jon time with Emily if they were going to form a bond. It was that bond that scared Alicia most of all.

An hour or so later, she heard the front door open and Jon call down the steps, "We're back." She sagged with relief and could concentrate on her work with her full attention. After she finished the first design, she went upstairs to find Emily. She was outside with Jon, watching him as he fitted the last section of paneling in the playhouse.

Alicia hugged her daughter and held her tight. "How was the playground?"

Emily squirmed out of her hold. "Fun. Mr. Wescott slid down the sliding board!"

"Oh, he did?"

"Yep. And he got stuck. I had to go up to the top and push him. We slid down together."

Jon ducked out of the playhouse, bare-chested. Alicia's gaze went directly to the strip of black hair down the middle. It looked so soft, his skin so bronze and taut...

"Apparently I was the first one down the sliding board today." He turned around and tried to brush off his backside where two dusty streaks on his navy slacks made her more aware of him than ever. His broad back was as intriguing as his chest. Drops of perspiration gleamed on his spine.

As she followed it up to his dark head, her gaze collided into his. "I, uh...see." Amusement sparked in his green eyes as he turned to face her, and she tried to control the rush of blood to her cheeks. "Are you making progress?" he asked.

She cleared her throat, feeling hot and bothered and not wanting him to know. "Yes. Yes, I am," she repeated with more certainty. "I'll soon be ready to start the second design."

"Two? And he picks one? Isn't that extra work?"

"If I'd done that the first time, this wouldn't have happened. Or at least if it had, I would have had another to fall back on. No work is ever wasted. I'll be able to use the design he doesn't choose for something else eventually."

"You're a perfectionist."

"I take pride in my work." She still tried to do everything to the best of her ability. It was an old habit formed so her father wouldn't criticize her.

"So do I. Come here a minute." He waved her into the playhouse.

Jon had finished paneling the last corner and it looked like a professional job. "It looks fantastic. You'll be done in no time."

His shoulder brushed her arm as he stooped to pick up his shirt hanging over the open window. His hot skin touching hers jolted her; she was rooted to the spot. When he straightened, he stared at her for a moment, his gaze going to her mouth. His regard made her break out in goose bumps and she nervously brushed her hair behind her ear.

"I'd better get back in," she murmured, still unable to move.

He reached out and skimmed his thumb over her lips. She shivered, though she was anything but cold. She could smell him, feel him, and heavens, she wanted to taste him. What was wrong with her?

"I still have the molding to attach," he said, a raspy inflection edging his words. "Do you mind if I take Emily with me to the lumberyard?"

She concentrated on the question rather than the current zipping between them. "As long as you keep a close watch on her."

"You know I will."

Suddenly she did know he would. Emily was becoming as important to him as she already was to Alicia. Yet the thought also scared her as well as comforted her. Out in the sunshine again, she took in a deep breath. Spring. Warm, balmy and waiting. Waiting for what?

Jon ducked out after her and pulled his shirt over his head. "We won't be long."

His arms were so long; his legs were so long. He was too much man for her to deal with right now. She went over to her daughter on the swing, kissed her on her forehead and explained what a lumberyard was, directing her to stay close to Mr. Wescott. With a grin as wide as her face, Emily agreed, looking as if she was poised on the verge of a new adventure.

Alicia suddenly realized it wasn't only her daughter who felt that way.

Chapter Five

Alicia smelled something. Something good. Her nose twitched as she sat at her desk and finished scanning the first design into the computer. The aroma made her stomach grumble. Taking her pencil in hand, she reminded herself that she didn't have time to think about food. But then the door opened at the top of the steps, causing the smell to become more potent, and her stomach grumbled again.

Jon carried a plate and a glass of water down the steps. "Supper is served, madam," he said in a butler's voice as he set the plate in front of her.

"Steak? Jon, what did you do? Emily doesn't even like steak."

"Do you?" he asked, towering over her.

"Of course, I do but—"

"Then enjoy it. Emily's got her hands on a hamburger she can't get into her mouth." He grinned.

"Someone will have to teach her steak is far superior to burgers."

Alicia laughed. "She'll never accept that."

Jon took a rolled napkin from his pants pocket and handed it to her. "Silverware. Corn on the cob is cooling. By the time you finish this, it'll be ready. Butter and salt?"

She felt overwhelmed and answered automatically, "Just butter. But, Jon..."

He pointed to her plate. "Eat. We'll save dessert for when you're finished for the night."

She took in a breath and took in him—male and sun and hard work. "Dessert?"

"We stopped at the bakery. Emily said you like lemon meringue pie as much as she does."

Alicia sighed and shook her head. "Are you spoiling her?"

He grinned, looking roguish and amused. "I hope so. Don't you like lemon meringue pie?"

Trying to keep her distance, Alicia said, "I thought bachelors didn't know how to cook."

"That's a misconception. If I ate out every night, I'd have constant indigestion. I like good plain food and I can cook that."

A small but loud voice came down the steps. "Mr. Wescott, Mr. Wescott, I'm ready for corn now."

Alicia started to rise to her feet. "She can get demanding if you let her. I'd better talk to her."

Settling his hand on her shoulder, he gently kept her in her chair. "She's testing her boundaries. Give her some latitude. You work. And don't worry. We'll be fine."

That reassurance bothered Alicia more than it comforted her. "I'll be up to put her to bed."

He gave her a long, probing look. "All right. We're going outside after supper to work on the playhouse. I'll let you know when we come in." He turned to walk away.

Reflexively she caught his arm. Her fingers pressed into his warm tan flesh and his hair tickled her.

Surprise registered on his face.

Quickly releasing him, she felt a warm flush heat her cheeks. "Thank you. I really appreciate this."

"It's my pleasure. By the way, six boxes were delivered by someone named Butch. He said the folding machine broke down again and can't be fixed till the end of the week."

Glancing down at her desk calendar, she saw her notation. "Shoot. I forgot Doug was sending those fliers over today. And now I'll have to fold them." She closed her eyes for a moment. "I'll deal with them in the morning...or afternoon."

"When do they have to be ready?"

Almost smiling at the purpose in his voice, she imagined he managed his business dealings with a tight rein and expectation that kept his employees scurrying. "Day after tomorrow."

The silence between them made Alicia more aware of the fact that his pants leg grazed her leg, and that he was still close enough to touch. His green eyes seemed to be trying to capture everything about her.

Finally Jon waved to Alicia's plate. "You'd better get started. Steak's much better hot than cold. I'll bring down the corn after Emily finishes."

Alicia watched him as he climbed the stairs. It had been a long time since anyone had taken care of her, had thought about her needs. Even though she and Ria depended on each other, especially for moral support, they'd both learned at a young age to be independent. Neither of them wanted to end up like their mother.

Alicia cut her steak and saw that it had been grilled medium-well, the way she liked it. She took a bite and swallowed, unable to wipe Jon's grin from her memory.

She went upstairs when she heard the screen door slam around eight-thirty. As Jon put his tools and supplies in the garage, she helped Emily wash up and get dressed for bed. Her daughter related everything she'd done that day, and everything Jon had accomplished.

He peeked in to say good-night while Alicia was reading Emily a story. Emily mumbled a sleepy good-night with her eyelids half closed.

Jon smiled. "So her energy *is* limited."

"Did she tire you out?" Alicia teased.

He leaned against the doorjamb. "More than a day at the office. But I'll get used to it. Do you mind if I take a shower?"

Jon naked in her bathroom. Alicia suddenly had a vivid picture she quickly banished. "You don't have to stay," she said, wishing he would, yet not sure she wanted to handle the situation that might arise if he did.

Crossing one ankle over the other, he shrugged. "We can have dessert together when you're finished working. You've been at it all day. You need some time to unwind. Unless you'd rather do it alone."

She could send him away. She could at least put his disturbing presence out of her life for tonight. But he was right. It would be good to unwind with someone, to relax over a cup of decaf. "If you don't mind staying, that would be nice. I'll get you a towel in a few minutes."

By the time Alicia finished the story, Emily was asleep. Kissing her daughter on the forehead, Alicia settled Emily under the covers and turned off the light.

Jon had stepped into the hall and was waiting—tall, male and imposing. He made her house seem much smaller. Scooting by him, she opened the linen closet and took out a blue towel and washcloth. "Do you need anything else?"

His green eyes snared hers. "Not right now. How about you?"

A wave of questions entered Alicia's mind at his words. Did she need him in her life? Did she need another brush of his lips across hers? Did she need more? The pull of him, the urge to lean into him and be closed into his arms was stronger than anything she'd ever felt. But years of caution led her to reply, "I need to get this job finished. If Emily calls for me, let me know."

He nodded, and denying the sudden need to be held against him and feel his lips on hers, she went back to work.

But Jon was difficult to put out of her mind. At her desk she heard the shower go on. In her mind's eye, she could see Jon shrug out of his shirt as he had that night at the spigot. All too well, she remembered his bronze skin and bare chest.

She closed her eyes as if that could block out the picture in her mind. She'd never been the type to ogle men, to even think about ogling men. Why start now?

Alicia concentrated on the logo in front of her, the tennis racket, archery bow and canoe she was determined to make work as an emblem.

By ten-thirty she'd faxed her client the logos. By eleven he'd called with his choice. Breathing a sigh of relief, she shut down the computer and shuffled her papers into a pile. Tomorrow morning she'd shoot it and get it to the printer. Taking a last look around to make sure everything was turned off and in place, she locked her office door and went upstairs. The hum of the television drew her towards the living room.

She stepped into the room, expecting to see Jon watching the news. Instead she found him stretched out on the couch, his feet bare, his eyes closed, his breathing even. The coffee table was stacked with folded fliers. He'd finished almost five boxes, then apparently had decided to take a break.

As she approached him, she could see he was sleeping. He'd changed from his polo shirt into a pale blue oxford, but hadn't bothered to button it. He'd said something about keeping an extra shirt in his car. Was he always prepared for everything?

Jon looked different sleeping. Younger, more approachable. The rise and fall of his chest kept her mesmerized. The black curly hair was so tempting. If she touched it, what would happen?

She needed to thank him for being such a help today. He didn't have to be involved in her life, just to be involved in Emily's. She almost wished he had a reason to be here other than to see Emily. That was crazy. The only other reason would be a relationship with her. Could she even consider that? With a man like Jon?

He was determined and willful, but he appeared to be considerate, too. He seemed to try to understand her wants and ideas. Trusting Patrick had been easy. Trusting a man like Jon... She didn't even really know him but she was beginning to.

Alicia couldn't help pushing his hair from his temple. She couldn't keep from leaning forward and dropping a gentle kiss of thanks above his brow. And she couldn't disregard the leap of her pulse and the tightening in her belly as she moved away, honestly hoping at that moment, he'd awaken.

But he didn't and she had to smile. She knew first-hand how tiring Emily could be. Alicia took the cream afghan from the back of the sofa and spread it out over Jon. She didn't have the heart to wake him. There was nothing wrong with him spending the night on her sofa. And in the morning, she'd make him the best breakfast he'd ever tasted.

Jon awakened to a stream of sunlight streaking across his face and the aroma of bacon in the air. His mouth watered and for a moment he wondered where he was. Only for a moment.

An afghan covered his legs, though half of it had fallen onto the carpet. He didn't remember pulling it from the back of the sofa. He did remember the brush of soft fingers, a wisp of a kiss. Had he been dreaming?

Sitting up, he put his feet flat on the floor and rubbed his hands over his face. The back door slammed and he heard Alicia call, "I'll see you at noon. Have a good day." A moment later, she stood in the doorway to the living room. "Breakfast is ready if you're hungry."

He was hungry, all right. For beautiful blue eyes, soft, pink lips, a figure with elegant curves. Jeez. In the rose jumpsuit she was wearing she looked good enough to—*Watch it, Wescott, or she'll throw you out before breakfast.* "I guess I conked out last night. Why didn't you wake me?" he asked.

"You looked so peaceful."

"I don't when I'm awake?"

She grimaced. "Hardly."

"And what do I look like when I'm awake?"

She laid her hand on the back of the sofa. "The truth?"

He nodded.

"Predatory."

Her answer bothered him. "That's how you see me?"

"You asked."

Yes, he had. And one thing he'd quickly learned about Alicia was that she was honest. Because he knew that, he asked, "Did you kiss me last night?"

Her face flushed to match her outfit.

He flipped the afghan to the side of his foot and patted the sofa next to him. "Come here."

She hesitated a moment, then did as he'd asked. But she sat on the edge, and he could tell she was nervous.

"Did I imagine it?"

She didn't look at him but at the fliers on the coffee table. "No. It was an impulse. I don't know what came over me . . . gratitude, I guess."

She was still denying the chemistry between them. "Are you sure it was gratitude?"

"Of course."

She'd answered much too quickly. He took her chin in his palm and turned her face to him. "It was a very nice expression of gratitude."

"Speaking of gratitude, I'd like to cook you dinner tonight. To properly thank you."

He suppressed a smile and dropped his hand. "Of course, we must do it properly." He wanted nothing more than to kiss her silly at the moment, but she was so nervous that he decided against it. She needed to be around him more so she could see he wasn't "predatory."

She hopped up from the sofa. "Your eggs are getting cold."

"Can't have that." He stood, too, and she took a step back. Giving her the room she needed, he stayed put. "I thought I'd put the shingles on the playhouse roof today."

"Don't you have business to take care of?"

He wasn't sure if her tone meant she didn't want him around or she was surprised he was staying. "I'll go back to the hotel after breakfast and make some calls. I was thinking about later this afternoon. I can probably finish before dark."

"I have a mother's group meeting this afternoon. We meet while our children go to gymnastics."

"Is Emily training for the Olympics?"

"No, she's learning to channel her energy. She loves tumbling."

Seeing the concerned expression on Jon's face, Alicia smiled. "The instructors are very careful. Right now, the kids are learning cartwheels." Picking up the afghan from the floor, she flipped it in half.

Jon took the other end to even it out and helped her fold it once more. His hands met hers. He brushed his fingertips against hers, then moved away. A little at a time, a touch here and there. She'd get used to him.

As Alicia laid the afghan on the back of the sofa, Jon frowned. Once she was used to him, then what did he want?

Jon swiped at his brow with his wrist and went in the back door to the kitchen for a glass of water. Hearing women's voices, he paused before he turned on the spigot.

One of the women said, "I don't know what to do with Barry. He's so defiant. No matter what I ask him to do, he does the opposite."

Another woman suggested, "He probably wants your attention. Aren't you spending a lot of time with Cindy's Girl Scouts?"

"That's true. We have an overnight camping trip coming up and he can't go along."

"Maybe he's feeling left out. I know Tim did when I took Jenny to her dance classes and the parades she performed in. They fight for equal time one way or another."

"I don't know how you do it, Alicia. Parenting is tough enough. Being a single parent has got to be the pits. Where do you find the stamina to run your own business and take care of everything else, too? The bills, the laundry, the car, the meals."

Alicia quietly answered. "I take it as it comes. Just as all of you do."

"Has Emily had any more stomachaches?"

"No. Not since I talked to her teacher about Jimmy teasing her at snack time about her grapes. Mrs. Edmunds did a lesson with them on nutritional foods and how candy bars don't have to be the snack of choice. Many of the kids are bringing fruit now, so Emily feels more comfortable."

"They want to conform. Even at their age."

Jon had listened intently to the conversation. He supposed he'd never realized exactly what was involved in being a parent, although he'd spent time with Adam and his children. It wasn't simply a matter of playing with a child, or buying him or her food and clothing. It was so much more. Twenty-four-hour responsibility for another life. And to do it alone had to be damn difficult.

Cecile had looked at the whole picture and found she didn't have the courage to face it. He would have helped her. He would have raised Emily himself.

But then his daughter never would have had Alicia for a mother.

HOW TO VALIDATE
YOUR
EDITOR'S FREE GIFT
"THANK YOU"

1. Peel off gift seal from front cover. Place it in space provided at right. This automatically entitles you to receive four free books and a beautiful Porcelain Trinket Box.

2. Send back this card and you'll get brand-new Silhouette Romance™ novels. These books have a cover price of $2.99 each, but they are yours to keep absolutely free.

3. There's no catch. You're under no obligation to buy anything. We charge nothing—ZERO—for your first shipment. And you don't have to make any minimum number of purchases—not even one!

4. The fact is thousands of readers enjoy receiving books by mail from the Silhouette Reader Service™ months before they're available in stores. They like the convenience of home delivery and they love our discount prices!

5. We hope that after receiving your free books you'll want to remain a subscriber. But the choice is yours—to continue or cancel, anytime at all! So why not take us up on our invitation, with no risk of any kind. You'll be glad you did!

6. Don't forget to detach your FREE BOOKMARK. And remember...just for validating your Editor's Free Gift Offer, we'll send you FIVE MORE gifts, *ABSOLUTELY FREE!*

YOURS FREE!

*This beautiful porcelain box is topped with a lovely bouquet of porcelain flowers, perfect for holding rings, pins or other precious trinkets — and is yours **absolutely free** when you accept our no risk offer!*

™

SILHOUETTE®

*WITH OUR
COMPLIMENTS*

THE EDITORS

THE SILHOUETTE READER SERVICE™: HERE'S HOW IT WORKS

Accepting free books places you under no obligation to buy anything. You may keep the books and gift and return the shipping statement marked "cancel". If you do not cancel, about a month later we will send you 6 additional novels, and bill you just $2.44 each plus 25¢ delivery and applicable sales tax, if any.* That's the complete price, and—compared to cover prices of $2.99 each—quite a bargain! You may cancel at any time, but if you choose to continue, every month we'll send you 6 more books, which you may either purchase at the discount price...or return at our expense and cancel your subscription.

*Terms and prices subject to change without notice. Sales tax applicable in N.Y.

Jon thought about that as he attached shingles to the playhouse roof, as he ate a wonderful home-cooked dinner of roasted chicken, baked potatoes, green beans and apple cobbler. He thought about it as Emily told him all about her gymnastics class, as he watched Alicia's lips curve around each forkful of her food, as he listened to her talk with her daughter as if she was a real person, not a miniature adult to be tolerated.

When Emily ran outside to play after dinner, he helped Alicia clear the table.

She dumped silverware into its holder in the dishwasher. "You don't have to do this if you want to finish the roof."

He tossed napkins into the trash bin in the cabinet under the sink. "I have another hour of light. And there's always tomorrow. Did you finish everything you intended to do today?"

Nodding, Alicia lined up the dishes in a neat row. "Yes. Doug called a little while before dinner. The pamphlets and business cards for the sports store are finished. We managed it after all."

"You had doubts?"

She stopped and took the dessert plates from the sink. "When I was in the middle of it last night, I did. And even with printing, Doug tries to accommodate me, but it's not always possible."

Jon was beginning to wonder about this "Doug" she spoke of. Was it just a professional relationship? It sounded as if it was. "Do you always use the same printer?"

She added the dessert plates to the bottom rack. "I've known Doug since grade school. When I worked at Mid State Textile designing fabrics before I was married, he printed our advertising material. I've never had a reason not to use him."

Jon kept his tone interested but casual. "His prices are comparable to other printers in the area?"

"Yes, and he doesn't try to hike them up on me. I trust him."

Absorbing that, Jon waited until she pushed in the bottom rack, then he loaded the last glass into the dishwasher. "I overheard you and the other mothers talking this afternoon."

Glancing at him sideways, she took a box of dishwasher detergent from under the sink. "And?"

"I decided Cecile giving up Emily for adoption might not have been such a bad thing."

Alicia's face showed her astonishment. "Just what did you hear?"

He shrugged, taking the soap powder from her and pouring it into its receptacle. "It wasn't what I heard, but what I realized. Parenting is a tough job. It requires dedication and focus. Cecile had both but they concerned her work. A child would have been shortchanged. I could see her hiring a nanny, not getting home from the office until after the child was in bed. I can't imagine Emily being raised like that."

Retrieving the box from him, Alicia mechanically stowed it in the cupboard. "But you would have stepped in."

She seemed as certain of that as he was. "Yes, I would have. But with us not being together, maybe shuffling Emily back and forth, she wouldn't have had the wonderful basis for adulthood that you've given her. I'm grateful for that, Alicia."

Her hands and body went still, and she didn't seem to know how to accept his compliment. Ducking her head and closing the dishwasher door, she murmured, "Thank you."

He put his hands on her shoulders and slowly nudged her around. And in that moment, he couldn't resist her, he couldn't back off. Her skin was too creamy, her hair too soft, her lips too sweetly curved. But the expression in her eyes perplexed him.

He braced his arms on either side of her on the counter. "Why are you afraid of me?"

Her chin lifted. "I'm not."

"Alicia." Her name was a slow caress.

Her eyelashes fluttered on her cheeks, then she confessed, "All right. Maybe I am. I'm not used to a man like you."

He couldn't understand her. He couldn't understand what made him different from . . . her husband, for example. "What kind of man do you think I am?"

She looked at his arms on either side of her. "The kind who takes what he wants. Look at us now. You've trapped me."

Trapped? In a flash, he'd lifted his arms away from her. "I didn't have you trapped. All you had to do was move."

"And now you're angry," she said in a low voice, as if that was even worse.

He quickly ran his hand through his hair. "You're wrong. I'm not angry. I'm trying to understand how you feel. I've never given you any indication I'd do anything to harm you."

She glanced at him out of lowered lids. "Except threats to take Emily."

"At the beginning when I didn't know the kind of mother you were, I intended to file for custody. But that's changed. We're working things out."

"Is that why you kissed me before? Because we're working things out?"

Damn the woman. Even now without touching her a passionate heaviness filled him, and it had nothing to do with Emily. "I kissed you because I wanted to kiss you, because I want to kiss you a lot harder and a lot deeper and I realize with you I'll have to get there in stages."

Her eyes widened and flashed silver sparks. "Stages? What am I? Some sort of project? A challenge?" She paused, then crossed to the table, grabbing the vinyl tablecloth. "You've just proved my point. Everything with you is calculated, and I'll never be sure of your motives."

His confusion flared into anger. "Everything's calculated is it? Well, how about this?"

Pulling her into his arms, tablecloth and all, he set his lips on hers. He didn't know if he'd caught her off guard or if she simply wanted the kiss as much as he did. After a moment of stillness, her lips molded and pressed against his. Her willingness banished his anger as well as the fleeting thought he might have made matters worse.

The vinyl tablecloth crinkled as he pressed her closer. Unable to feel her against him, he stroked his hand up and down her back. Her lips opened and he took advantage of the gift. She was sweetness and fire and so different from any woman he'd ever kissed. She was shy, yet assertive, vulnerable, yet strong willed. It all showed in her kiss as she tentatively met his tongue, then boldly stroked it.

Groaning, he cradled her with his other hand and tilted her head, taking the kiss deeper. He felt her fingers creep up the back of his neck and delve into his hair. His hands shook and he realized a woman's response had never done that to him before.

He needed air. He needed to absorb this chemistry teasing him, enticing him, leading him into an impulsive situation that could backfire. Raising his head, he waited for her to open her eyes. When she did, he saw the fire of passion still burning. It almost made him kiss her again. Before he could even think about it, she withdrew her arm from his shoulder and took a step back, gripping the tablecloth tightly with her other hand.

"I'm not sure whether to apologize or not," he said ruefully.

She gazed at him with steady eyes. "Are you sorry about it?"

"No."

"Then I guess you have nothing to apologize for."

He wished she wouldn't keep her feelings hidden so well. "I said I'd wait until you wanted me to kiss you."

"I wanted you to kiss me," she said softly.

He wanted more from her than that. "Did you enjoy it?"

"I'm not sure 'enjoy' is the right word."

"What is the right word?" he pressed.

"I don't know. The world spun. I felt hot and cold and everything in between." She smiled. "Let me think about it a while, then I'll tell you if I enjoyed it."

He laughed and wanted to kiss her again. A longer kiss that would lead them— He cut off the thought and gave her a hug instead. She wrapped her arms around him and returned it, and he couldn't remember when a hug had been so satisfying.

Alicia was preparing invoices the next morning when her office doorbell rang. Her breath caught. Jon hadn't said he'd be dropping in today. When he'd left last night, he'd placed a chaste kiss on her forehead. After that explosive kiss in her kitchen, she'd been, well—she might as well admit it—disappointed.

Rising from her desk, she went to answer the door. She didn't understand her feelings any more than she understood her behavior. She was both fascinated by Jon and wary of him. He'd kissed her in anger, yet he hadn't stayed angry. He'd been demanding, but gentle, too. Weren't men either angry, demanding and selfish or flexible, gentle and passive? She'd never known a mix. But then she hadn't known many men, not before Patrick and not since. She dealt with men consistently in business circumstances, but that was on the surface only; she was good at hiding behind reserve.

The young man standing at her door smiled broadly. "Delivery for Alicia Fallon."

Her mouth dropped open.

"Surprises are nice, aren't they?" he asked pleasantly holding out the vase she'd admired at the antique shop. It was filled with lilacs, yellow day lilies, pink sweetheart roses and baby's breath.

Carefully she took the vase from him. The delivery man gave her a final smile and ran to the florist's truck parked at the curb. Alicia carried the flowers inside. Her fingers trembled as she took the small envelope from the plastic holder and opened it.

Thanks for dinner. And the kiss.

Jon

He was slipping past her reserve.

Gently running her fingers over the iris pattern on the glass, she wondered if he was this thoughtful with everyone. She wondered . . .

The phone rang. Before she picked up the receiver, she took a long whiff of the lilacs and smiled as she said, "Hello. Designs For You."

A woman's voice on the other end of the line asked, "Is Jonathan Wescott there?"

Why would anyone think Jon was there? Unless it was his secretary or someone he'd given the number to. "No, he's not. This is Alicia Fallon. Can I help you?"

"I'm Valerie Sentara, Mrs. Fallon, from the *West Coast Sentinel*. I'm looking for information."

"What kind of information?"

"As you probably know, Jonathan Wescott is of interest to many of our readers. I need a tidbit or two for my column this week. Is it true he's purchasing a Harrisburg newspaper?"

"How did you get my number?"

"I have my sources, Mrs. Fallon. Can you tell me if my information is correct?"

"No, I can't." Alicia hadn't had much experience with reporters, but she knew enough to watch her words. This woman was fishing, and Alicia didn't want to give her any bait.

"Surely you can tell me if he's interested in purchasing one."

"No, I can't."

"What can you tell me, Mrs. Fallon?"

"I'm afraid I don't have any information for you."

"Then why is Mr. Wescott having brochures printed with your company?"

Apparently Ms. Sentara didn't know she and Jon had a nonbusiness connection. "You'd have to ask him that."

"Yes, well, Mr. Wescott is under the impression that he doesn't have to inform the public about his business dealings. Anyone who owns ten newspapers and varied other interests in communities is accountable to the people he affects. Are you sure you can't give me any information?"

Ten newspapers? Varied other interests? Jon possessed a lot more status and wealth than she'd imagined. She didn't want to seem defensive or the reporter would sense she was holding back. The less she said, the better. "I'm positive."

The reporter paused. "All right. But let me give you my number in case you get any information." The woman's voice lowered conspiratorially. "In fact, if you do, I could make it worth your while." She rattled off her number.

Alicia didn't bother to write it down. When she hung up the phone, she stared at the flowers, at the vase she'd determined was too expensive for her budget.

Taking the beautiful glassware in her hands again, she appreciated its elegance and the loveliness of the flowers. She thought about Jon's kiss and the way it had made her feel. Was the vase really a gift of gratitude? Or was it another strategy?

Chapter Six

Alicia had called to thank him for the flowers and the vase, and had been polite. Jon knew her well enough to realize that when she was polite, she was protecting herself. Did she think he was trying to buy her?

He'd given presents to women before. Much more expensive presents than that vase. And they'd always responded favorably—especially when they'd been involved in a relationship. Was that what Alicia meant by trading favors? He'd truly simply wanted to thank her. Hadn't he? Jeez, she had him questioning his own motives!

Suspecting time would only put distance between them, he decided a visit would be less threatening to Alicia during the day because her free time would be limited. He approached her backyard knowing she usually took the hour after lunch to play with Emily. But mother and daughter weren't in the yard. He heard voices coming from the kitchen and went to the back door.

Emily's usually excited voice sounded tearful and sad.
Jon didn't bother to knock.

Alicia was sitting at a chair at the table, Emily by her
side, her finger in her mouth, the streak of tears down her
cheeks. Unable to stop himself, he went over and
crouched down beside her. "What's wrong, honey?"

Alicia gave him a look he couldn't interpret. But her
voice was politely cool as she said, "Jon, Emily and I
have something to settle. Maybe it would be better if you
gave us a few minutes."

She didn't have to take care of everything alone anymore, and he wouldn't be shut out of his daughter's life.
As tactfully as he could, he suggested, "Maybe two heads
are better than one."

Alicia brushed Emily's hair away from her eyes. "Do
you want to tell Mr. Wescott what's wrong?"

The child didn't hesitate. "I didn't get my turn at the
computer. I didn't get a turn yesterday, either. Mark did.
And Jenny did."

Her lower lip trembled and Jon's heart melted. "Why
didn't you get a turn?"

"'Cause Mark used it, then we had to sit in a circle,
and Jimmy used it, then we had snacks, then Jenny used
it and it was time to go home!"

Alicia explained, "The school district just bought two
computers for the kindergarten. And of course the children can't use them at just anytime when their teacher is
teaching. They have to wait their turn. There are twenty-
five in the class, and I'm trying to explain to Emily that
this is just like waiting her turn to slide down the big
sliding board if the playground is crowded. Only this wait
is longer. It might be a few days until she gets her chance
at the computer."

"Only two computers? Why aren't there more?"

Alicia stroked her daughter's hair but sat up straight in her chair. "Because schools have cutbacks just like everyone else. Computers aren't a necessity in kindergarten."

"But she could learn so much faster!"

Alicia gave him an annoyed look. With a nod at Emily, and in a lowered voice she said, "You're not helping."

He knew he was a problem solver; he wouldn't apologize for that. And he could see an easy solution to this problem. Putting his arm around Emily's shoulders, he said, "Your mom's right, honey. For now. It's like standing in line to get a hamburger at McDonald's. You just have to wait."

His daughter's pretty green eyes met his and her voice was resigned. "If you say so." She turned to Alicia. "Can't you talk to Mrs. Edmunds so I can have a turn tomorrow?"

"I'll bet Mrs. Edmunds has a list with everybody's name. What you could do tomorrow is ask her how many names are before yours. Then you'd know what day you can have your turn. Okay?"

Emily nodded. *"O-kay."* Turning to Jon, she asked him, "Are you gonna work on my playhouse?"

"Not right now. I'd like to talk to your mom for a little while."

Alicia tucked Emily's hair behind her ears. "Why don't you go get your letter board and take it downstairs? I'll be down in a few minutes."

Emily ran into the living room and scampered up the stairs to her room. Jon rose to his feet and waited until she was out of earshot. "She shouldn't have to wait. She should be in a school that will give her the opportunities she deserves. She's a bright child, Alicia."

"Don't you think I know that?" she answered defensively. "Waiting her turn to use a computer won't dim her intelligence. It'll teach her she can't have everything when she wants it."

He went to the living room and glanced up the stairs, then paced back to Alicia. "And I say she needs to be challenged in a forward-looking school, one where she'll get individual attention and can progress at her own rate. There are several of them in the L.A. area and—"

Alicia stood. "And what?"

Jon didn't even realize it had been an idea in his mind. Yet, eventually the subject would have come up. "Maybe you should consider moving to Los Angeles where we could put Emily in one of the best private schools in the country. I have a friend on the board."

If possible, Alicia's ramrod-straight posture became even straighter. "I imagine you do."

In his best boardroom persuasive manner, he pushed further. "There's always a niche for your kind of business. I'd be glad to back you. We need good graphic artists on the West Coast, too. With your talent and skills, I could always get you a job on one of the papers if you'd rather do that."

Emily came scurrying through the kitchen and hopped down the steps to the lower level.

Alicia clasped her hands in front of her and steadily pinned Jon with her gaze. "How long have you had this planned out?"

The suspicions were back in her blue eyes. Jamming his hands into his pockets, he insisted, "I didn't have it planned out. But it certainly would solve a lot of problems, wouldn't it? I would be near Emily and so would you."

"It will solve *your* problems. I have a life here, Jon. I not only have a business that has taken time to build, but I have friends. So does Emily. And Ria's here. I don't think you have any idea how difficult it would be for us to leave her."

"Even if that's what's best for Emily?"

Alicia's hand waved through the space between them in frustration. "Treating her like one of the privileged few and giving her anything she wants is not what's best for her. There's nothing wrong with public school, waiting her turn and learning the world doesn't revolve around her. We've known you two weeks and already you're trying to run our lives!"

Taking his hands from his pockets, he went to the window and stared at Emily's swing set and the playhouse that had provided him the opportunity to get to know her. "I want to be near my daughter. I want her to have everything I can give her. What's so wrong with that?"

Alicia's voice soared over his shoulders. "What's wrong is that I've spent the past two years since Patrick died trying to give her a stable life. You talk about moving as if we can just pick up and make a change overnight. You're asking us to give up an awful lot. What are you giving up?"

He faced her then and boardroom persuasion was forgotten. "What do you want me to do? Move here? My headquarters are in Los Angeles. I'm offering to make you comfortable and give Emily the things you can't."

Alicia's expression didn't soften; neither did her determination. "*Things* aren't what she needs, Jon. She needs security and love. She has that here." Shaking her head, she added, "I suspected that vase would come with strings. I was right."

Her implication made him see red. "No, you were not right. I purchased that vase because you liked it. And that's the only reason. I wanted to give you something you obviously couldn't give yourself. You think about that, and then you think about how you'd feel if your daughter were living three thousand miles away. If you don't seriously consider moving to California, joint custody might be a necessity. So think about that before you decide your life is too good to change."

He strode to the back door and left, his heart heavy. The idea of not seeing his daughter for months at a time was a reality he didn't want to contemplate.

Alicia brushed Emily's hair the next morning as she helped her get ready for school. Taking a pink barrette from the dresser, she clipped it in her daughter's hair.

"Mommy, is Mr. Wescott comin' over today?"

If she wasn't thinking about Jon, Emily mentioned him. "I don't know, honey."

"He's gonna do my playhouse, isn't he?"

"You mean finish it?"

"Uh-huh."

"I'm not sure."

"He didn't say goodbye."

No, he certainly didn't. Alicia had gone over their conversation in her head. She'd thought about what Jon had said, rather than focusing on the ever-present threat of a custody suit. Trying to put herself in his position, she asked herself, *What if I'd found my daughter after five years and she lived across the country?*

Adjusting Emily's barrette until it was straight, Alicia wondered if she had overreacted. The bottom line was that she didn't want any man controlling her life the way her father had controlled her mother's. But was Jon just trying to get his own way or did he truly want what was best for Emily? For all of them.

It was a hard call to make, and she supposed she had to get to know him better before she could judge his motives. For now, she should give him the benefit of the doubt. But he also had to realize he was asking her to change her life, to give up people and a place she held dear, especially Ria.

She and her sister had only been separated during college. Alicia had enrolled in the Columbus Art Institute and Ria had won a scholarship to Northwestern. Those five hours of traveling distance between them had taken forever when they could manage the bus fare. And they'd saved money from their jobs to make at least two lengthy phone calls a week. Alicia had almost felt as if a part of her was somewhere else.

So after they graduated, even though their mother had already relocated to her sister's, they'd come back to their childhood hometown and rented an apartment together. Then Alicia had met Patrick and the rest was history. Ria now lived in the first floor of the old Victorian house by herself.

Patrick had never been threatened by her relationship with her twin. How would Jon feel?

Emily squirmed under her mother's hands and Alicia knew she'd kept her daughter still for too long. She turned her around to face the mirror. "Well, what do you think?"

She made a face. "The barrette feels funny."

"Do you want me to take it out?"

Emily tilted her head. "No. It's okay."

After Alicia fed Emily breakfast and watched her run over to the neighbor who was driving for their car pool this week, her thoughts returned to Jon. She needed to see him. She needed to talk to him and not let bitterness or resentment grow between them that could hurt their daughter.

His hotel was across town and Alicia decided to drive there. The whole way over she tried to rehearse what she wanted to say. But each time, it came out differently.

Once at the hotel, Alicia checked Jon's suite number on the card he'd given her with his phone number. As she passed the front desk, the clerk looked over her lavender-and-blue blazer and tailored blue skirt and smiled. Taking the elevator to the fifth floor, she walked to the corner suite and knocked. No one answered.

A maid came out of the room next door.

Alicia knocked again. She realized she should have called first, but it was too late for hindsight.

The middle-age maid took a look at her and then another. "It's none of my business, but the man from that suite left with his gym bag about fifteen minutes ago. He goes to the gym most mornings."

Alicia smiled. "Thank you. I didn't know whether or not I should wait."

"You better not take too long to find him. That one's a looker. You don't see men like that much anymore, no indeed."

Alicia took the elevator to the second floor where the gym was located, mulling over the maid's words. Jon Wescott certainly attracted attention. He was that kind of man.

She found him at the free-weight stand facing the mirror, eyes closed in concentration as he lifted a weight above his head and lowered it again. Sweat gleamed on his forehead. Just watching his raw masculine power made Alicia catch her breath. She remembered his lips on hers, his arms surrounding her, his male scent intoxicating her.

He opened his eyes and saw her standing behind him. The nerve at his jaw twitched but other than that he didn't move. There was no glimmer of recognition in his gaze, no relaxing of his stance. He lifted the weight up and down again.

Alicia felt embarrassed, overdressed and downright nervous. She'd worked at becoming assertive all her adult life, but it was still difficult for her sometimes. Especially with someone like Jon.

Holding on to her courage with both hands, she asked, "Can we talk?"

Still he faced the mirror. "You seemed to have everything figured out the last time I saw you."

"I'm sorry if I overreacted." Her apology came out so softly, she was afraid he hadn't heard.

He settled the weight on its stand and faced her. "That's a start."

He was acting as if none of this was his fault. "Look, Jon, this isn't easy for me." Her gaze ran over him quickly, but not so quickly that she wasn't aware of every bare inch of him, every muscle, every annoyed vibration emanating from him. "If you'd rather I call and make an appointment..."

Suddenly the annoyance left his expression. "Lately I haven't made appointments with you, have I? I just barge in."

She diplomatically kept quiet.

Wiping his face with the towel on the weight stand, he stuffed it into his gym bag then picked up the duffel. "Let's go up to my suite. This is no place to carry on a conversation."

He started walking, obviously expecting her to follow. She did, but not at his fast clip. He slowed and turned, raising a brow. "Is there a problem?"

"Was that an order?"

He sighed and rubbed his hand over his face. "No, it wasn't an order—it was a practical suggestion. Do you have a better one?"

He might be irritated with her but she didn't deserve his sarcasm. "Did you get out of bed on the wrong side?"

"Actually I didn't get much sleep. Between the situation with you and a problem with contract negotiations at one of the papers, I might have managed an hour or two. So, you're right, I'll warn you right now, I'm not at my best. Do you want to meet later?"

"Will your disposition be any sweeter?" she asked with the same exasperation he was portraying.

He blew out a breath and shook his head. "Probably not."

"Then let's get this over with," she suggested blandly and started walking toward the door. Feeling his gaze on her back, she kept walking.

She heard him chuckle, then break into a laugh. Suddenly she felt better. They walked to the elevator side by side.

Jon let her into his suite, and she took a good look around. The room was decorated in a rich forest green, the carpet, the blue-and-green flowered spread and drapes, the love seat and chair. The kitchen was small but well equipped. The furniture seemed to be mahogany. She wondered if the desk was as heavy as it looked. It held a fax machine and laptop computer as well as a phone that was a mate to the one by the bed. The bed. King-size. Jon-size.

"What do you think?" he asked, opening the drapes.

"It's very nice."

Even with the drapes open, the miniblinds kept the room dim. "But it's not home," he stated.

Going over to the sofa, she ran her hand over the back. No worn places. No stains from spills. "I suppose it's not."

When he opened the blinds, the morning sunshine poured in. "I miss walks on the beach, the sound of the ocean, the cry of gulls. Funny what you get used to. You don't miss it until you don't have it."

"That's the problem, Jon. I do know what I have here. I know I'd miss it."

"I approached you all wrong yesterday."

"You didn't approach. You jumped in with both feet. Do you realize you didn't even knock before you came in? You took over with Emily as if you'd been doing it all her life. You suggested we turn our lives upside down. Then you expected me not to react, to calmly accept all of it?"

Jon's fax machine beeped. He went over to it as it spewed out a missive. With a frown, he threw the paper on the desk. Then he faced her, giving her his complete attention. "I did not have a scheme in mind, Alicia. I want you to move to California, but the vase had nothing to do with that."

Knowing she was playing with fire, especially with him dressed as he was, she took a few steps closer to Jon, because she needed to, because she needed for them to be friendly again. "I believe you. And I want to thank you again for the vase and the flowers. It's been a long time since anyone was that thoughtful." There hadn't been romance between her and her late husband. Just quiet friendship and a comfortable feeling that had made her feel safe from the first time she'd met him.

Jon smiled then, a slow, lazy, sexy smile that led her to dream of romance and dark nights and silk. It was an unfamiliar dream and scary in the excitement it aroused in her.

He straightened the lapel of her jacket. "I realize my suggestion is overwhelming. So I have another. What if you and Emily come to Los Angeles with me to look around? You can see my home, meet my mother, see the advantages I can give Emily. It would give you time to get used to the idea and give you a vacation at the same time. How much longer will Emily be in school?"

As his fingers slid over the blue ribbing, she wished he'd touch her skin instead. "She 'graduates' in a month, on June third."

He grinned and dropped his hand. "Big event."

She could see the small lines around Jon's eyes, almost feel the damp heat from his shirt. "You bet. They get to wear little mortarboards and everything."

"Am I invited?" he asked, his voice low and husky as his gaze centered on her lips.

She swallowed and tried to take a deep breath. But it was difficult. "I have a feeling Emily wouldn't want you to miss it. But will you still be here then?"

He ran his thumb across Alicia's chin and down her neck. She tried to keep her mind on the conversation as he said, "I can arrange it. Do *you* want me there?"

She moistened her dry lips and tried to find her voice. "I'd like you to come."

He'd almost closed the distance between them when he paused. "I need a shower. Why don't you think about a trip to L.A. and when it would be best for you to go. I know you have to plan ahead with your business. I'll only be five minutes." As he headed for the bathroom, his gaze fell on the fax. "Will you do me a favor?"

She nodded.

"I'm expecting a call from Adam Hobbs."

"Your lawyer?" Her chest tightened.

"This has nothing to do with Emily. It's business. If Adam calls, tell him I received a copy of the contract and I'll get back to him before five. California time. Got it?"

She smiled. "Got it."

Jon disappeared into the bathroom and her smile remained. They were getting along again. The tension was gone. Well, some of the tension. She had a feeling the knot in her stomach wouldn't diminish until he kissed her.

Jon had no sooner gotten into the shower when his phone rang. Alicia didn't hesitate to go to the desk and pick up the receiver. "Hello. Jon Wescott's room."

"Well, well. Mrs. Fallon, isn't it?"

Alicia recognized the voice. Valerie Sentara. She thought about slapping the receiver down again, but that could make matters worse. "Mr. Wescott is unavailable at the moment. May I take a message?"

"Yes. He knows why I'm calling. You tell him he'd better come clean or I'll dig up the story myself. Got it?"

"I'll give him the message, Ms. Sentara."

A few minutes later, Jon came out of the bathroom in cutoff denim shorts and a green T-shirt, his feet bare, his hair still damp after being toweled dry. Ignoring his potent male magnetism, Alicia stayed put on the sofa where she'd settled and worried. "You had a phone call. Valerie Sentara."

He went over to the dresser and took his wallet from a drawer, stuffing it into his back pocket. "A nuisance I have to deal with occasionally."

"She might be more than a nuisance. She called me the other day asking for information. She recognized my voice today."

He swore and spun around. "How the hell did she find out about you?"

Alicia lifted both hands in a vague gesture that said she didn't know. "She knew you'd come to me about the programs. She didn't know anything else."

"That information could have slipped from someone in my office," he muttered. "Damn the woman."

When Alicia couldn't stand the silence, she asked, "What are you going to tell her?"

He hiked a brow. "About?"

"Me. Emily. She wants to know what you're doing here." Alicia gave Jon the reporter's exact message.

Jon crossed to the sofa and sat beside her. Very close. "Only Adam, a lawyer here, and my mother know about you and Emily and my real reason for being in Camp Hill. And they aren't going to say a word. Believe me, Alicia, I don't want you and Emily in the middle of a scandal."

He was near enough to touch, near enough to kiss. But she was still worried. "But how can you stop her? She says she has sources."

"She's bluffing. Did you give her anything to go on?"

"No. But my being here—"

"Doesn't mean a thing. This could be a business meeting."

Jon seemed confident he could handle the reporter. And if no one but his lawyers and his mother knew the situation, they were safe. Alicia relaxed against the sofa. "*Could* be?"

He moved even closer and brushed his hand down her cheek. "I don't think of you as business, Alicia. In fact, sometimes I don't even think of you as Emily's mother."

Her heart thudded; his bare thigh tensing against her skirt alerted her to his next move. Slipping his arm around her shoulders, he turned her to him.

Teasingly he ran his finger along the round neck of her lavender shell. "How do you always manage to look so prim, yet so feminine at the same time?"

"Prim?" Her voice came out on a tiny breath.

He sensually rubbed his cheek against hers. "Mm-hmm. Unless you think I'm not looking. Unless I get too close. Unless I catch you off guard."

His taut skin against hers, his warm breath on her chin, the whiskey huskiness of his voice led her to tell him the truth. "I'm not feeling very prim right now."

He chuckled and slid his hand under her hair at the base of her neck. His long fingers appreciated the silky strands as he kissed the tip of her chin, the line of her jaw. He stopped to murmur, "I'm not being predatory right now, Alicia. I'm being a man. There's a difference. Do you want me to stop?" He nibbled the corner of her lip.

She was trying to keep her head clear. She was trying to hold onto... she forgot what she was trying to hold onto. All she could think about was Jon kissing her, and her kissing him back. "Not yet," she murmured, attempting to keep some control over the situation.

Pulling away slightly, his expression was serious. "You'll tell me when?"

She nodded.

Nudging her toward him with his hand, he nibbled at her lips a few seconds more before he pressed his mouth full against hers and waited. She knew what he was waiting for, and his patience melted any last remnants of re-

sistance. With a small sigh, she opened her lips and h
thrust inside.

The kiss was anything but patient. It was hot and de
manding and it awakened all her simmering fires. Sh
hadn't even known she was capable of fire. But from th
moment Jon had walked into her office, the foreign, slo
burning had begun. This man created turmoil, he cre
ated excitement, he created fear. But he also created a
incredible sense of longing, of wanting, and of needir
that had laid dormant all her life.

He tempted her to respond fully to him, and it didn
take any coaxing. She stroked her tongue against his an
felt him shudder. When she kneaded his shoulders, di
covering strength and muscle, then ran her hands dow
his upper arms, his whole body tensed. She had powe
over him!

The longer the kiss lasted, the more need curled insic
her. Sex had been pleasant with Patrick, but never pa
sionate, never consuming. He'd seemed to be intereste
in her more as a companion and then as a mother to h
child, than as a woman. And that had suited her just fin
Because she'd been afraid of any male dominance.

But Jon didn't dominate. He awakened. He excite
When he laid his hand on her breast, she'd never fe
more alive. But as he pushed her blazer aside, as h
molded his palm against her breast, the caution of a lif
time caught up to the swirling sensations that threatene
to overtake her. She covered his hand with hers an
pulled away, breaking off the kiss.

He stared at her for an intense moment, and sh
watched as he banked the flames leaping in his gaz
"When?" he asked, the question raspy.

She'd like nothing more than to let him kiss her agai
to feel his touch. But she'd only known him such a sho

time, and there were still so many issues to settle. "When," she repeated shakily.

He brought her hand to his lips and kissed the palm. "All right. Have you thought about California?"

She'd thought the kiss was just for her. She'd thought it had nothing to do with persuasion. But now she wasn't so sure. What he was asking was reasonable. Even if she didn't move out there, it would be good for Emily to become familiar with Jon's home and surroundings because she'd be visiting him eventually. Alicia realized how difficult that arrangement would be for her to accept. The thought of being parted from Emily made her heart ache. She had to seriously consider a trip to L.A.

Thinking about her schedule and the ebb and flow of business, Alicia said, "I could leave for a week or so in mid-June. Would that be all right? Even if you don't stay here that long, Emily and I could fly out."

He looked at the fax lying on the desk. "That would be a good time for you to be in L.A. You can go to the charity gala with me. And as far as staying till then, so far, I've been able to handle business from here. I might have to take a trip out before mid-June, but I won't plan to leave until you can fly back with me."

Before, she had feared his staying, now she looked forward to it. She definitely needed to talk to Ria.

Later that evening, after Jon had nailed the last shingle to the playhouse roof, had read his daughter a story and kissed Alicia with more restraint than he cared to use, he lifted the phone on his desk and called his mother.

"They're coming to L.A. in June," he told her.

"She accepts you as the child's father?"

"More and more. The results of the testing will settle it for her. Could you do me a favor?"

"You know I will."

"Find a toy store and buy everything you think a five-year-old will enjoy. Dolls, for sure. Maybe you can find one of those wooden dollhouses with the miniature furniture. She'd like that. I think she has an artistic bent so get drawing materials of all kinds—crayons, markers, pencils. Maybe an easel."

"Jon, she's five. And what will her mother think if you buy Emily a roomful of toys?"

He suspected how Alicia felt about presents. "I want my daughter to feel at home. Don't forget stuffed toys."

"Jon..."

"Mom, you're going to love them."

"Them?" She expectantly waited for an explanation.

"Alicia's special. She's different from other women I've known."

"From what you've told me she sounds like a good mother," Marilyn Wescott said cautiously.

"She's more than that," he mumbled to himself, only he made the mistake of letting his mother hear.

"Anything like Cecile?"

His mom knew how difficult the end with Cecile had been. She knew he'd seen his dreams go up in smoke. "She's nothing like Cecile." He thought about Alicia tucking Emily's hair behind her ear, laughing with Ria at the flower stand, sharing with other mothers. "She connects with people. You should see her with Emily. She has a twin sister and they're very close. She even collects depression glass from flea markets."

"Be careful, son."

"I've been careful a long time. After being with Emily and Alicia, I know I haven't been happy. Maybe it's time not to be so cautious."

"There's a child to think of."

"I know. I won't rush into anything, believe me." But then he thought about Alicia's blue eyes, her beautiful smile, the arousing feel of her in his arms.

After he hung up the phone, he repeated to himself, *Don't rush*. But he knew he wasn't the type to bide his time for long.

Chapter Seven

Alicia's house had almost become a second home to Jon. He'd been in Camp Hill almost seven weeks, though it didn't seem possible. Yet in other ways, it did. Any day now, they could expect the results from the DNA testing. Then he and Alicia could tell Emily he was her father.

In the past month, he'd gotten into the routine of working in his hotel suite during the day, spending each evening with Alicia and Emily. And weekends. They'd painted the exterior of the playhouse, visited Hersheypark, the National Zoo in D.C., had picnics with Ria, or simply watched videos with Emily. Once or twice a week, he'd surprise Alicia with lunch. He'd taken her to the movies, the theater and to dinner for two as often as he could convince her to let Ria or Gertie baby-sit. He enjoyed every moment with Alicia, every kiss, every touch. He'd been careful not to rush or crowd her, and always pulled away before the urge to sweep her into his arms and carry her to her bedroom overwhelmed him. A reticence in Alicia's response told him although she'd relaxed around him considerably, she might still not be sure about his motives. He didn't know how to teach her to trust him. Maybe going to L.A. and being on his home turf would help.

Los Angeles seemed a world away, but he was anxious to get back, to walk on the beach and try to sort out his feelings for Alicia. He couldn't imagine leaving her or Emily here while he returned to the West Coast. He'd just have to convince her that living in California had many more advantages than living in Pennsylvania. Maybe today they'd pick the best time to fly out. But first, he had to tell her he was going to miss Emily's graduation.

Once at the house, he realized that *not* knocking was now a habit. Opening Alicia's office door, he saw the room was empty. That was unusual for a Monday morning. The outside door wasn't locked, so he assumed she'd run upstairs for something. But as he stepped deeper into the room, he heard voices from the kitchen. One female voice, and one male.

He didn't think twice about calling up the stairs.

Alicia's voice came back lilting, with a smile in it. "C'mon up, Jon. There's someone I want you to meet."

The scene that met Jon was a little too cozy for his peace of mind—place settings for two, coffee, muffins and an attractive man a few years younger than himself sitting across from Alicia. The man had brown hair, brown eyes and a mustache that seemed to crown a smug smile.

Alicia's smile was relaxed and welcoming. "Jon Wescott, this is Doug Arigo."

Jon clenched his jaw and extended his hand. The printer Alicia often spoke with shook it then motioned to the breakfast he and Alicia were sharing. "Join us?"

Alicia took a mug from the wooden tree on the counter and filled it with coffee. "Doug brought the muffins and since we both skipped breakfast, we're taking a mid-morning break." She brushed past Doug to set Jon's coffee in front of him and didn't flinch when her arm brushed Doug's shoulder.

"So, Doug. Do you take breaks like this often?" Jon asked, his tight-lipped question a little too snappy.

Alicia's smile faltered and she glanced at him sharply.

Doug didn't seem to notice. "Licia and I don't get a chance to visit much anymore. We're both too busy."

Jon couldn't prevent his irritated frown. A pet name, too. "You know Alicia from high school, right?"

"Went through most of grammar school together, too."

"Did you date?"

"Jon!"

He knew he'd stepped across the boundary but didn't care. Doug Arigo was entirely too comfortable with Alicia. And worse yet, she seemed comfortable with him. Jon kept an expectant attitude in the silence that followed.

Doug shrugged nonchalantly and answered the question. "My crowd was too fast for Alicia. Mostly we passed in the hall and helped each other with algebra."

Alicia held the plate of baked goods in front of Jon's nose. "Muffin?"

Silver sparks danced in her blue eyes. She was so damn beautiful, and right now she was perturbed with him. "No, thanks. Coffee's fine. You know I prefer sweets with dinner or before bed."

Her eyes widened and she plopped the dish not so gently on the table.

Doug watched the interaction between them with interest. "I understand Licia's going to visit California with you."

"Alicia is going to stay at my house in Malibu. I'm hoping she and Emily will like California enough to stay."

Doug swung around to Alicia. "You might be leaving?"

"Nothing is settled," Alicia said with a straightening of her shoulders. She patted Doug's hand. "Any move won't be sudden. I'll give you plenty of notice... *if* it happens."

He turned his hand up under hers. "I'd miss you."

"I'd miss you, too. I'd have to call a real plumber to unclog my drain."

Doug laughed.

Jon cleared his throat, thoroughly uncomfortable with their easy touching.

Doug picked up his napkin and wiped his mouth. "I'd better get back."

Alicia closed the box of goodies. "Butch will be glad to see these."

"No, you keep them for Emily. She loves the cranberry and orange."

"I'll keep one of those for her, but you take the rest along. We don't need them."

Jon wanted to tell Doug he knew Emily liked cranberry-orange muffins. He wanted to tell this man who knew Alicia too well that he was Emily's father.

After Doug left, Alicia turned toward Jon and he knew she was going to blast him. "I know what you're going to say, so you don't have to say it," he concluded before she could fire the first shot.

She simply lifted her pretty dark blond brows.

"I was a bit proprietary."

She frowned.

"I was arrogant and proprietary."

"Would you like to tell me why?" she asked in the quiet manner he was becoming accustomed to.

"No, I wouldn't." As she opened her mouth to respond, he said in a low voice, "But I will. I was jealous."

She looked astonished. "Of Doug? Why? He and I hardly ever see each other."

"You talk on the phone often."

Her nose wrinkled in dismissal. "That's business."

Jon couldn't shake off the possessiveness that had attacked him as soon as he'd noticed Doug in her kitchen. "You don't treat him as if it's business. You smile at him, you depend on him, you touch him as if..."

"As if I've known him all my life," she filled in as she stacked one plate on top of another.

"That wasn't what I was going to say," he blurted out.

She waited.

"I want you to be that free around me." He couldn't believe the note of longing in his voice. He always initiated kissing or touching with Alicia. If only she felt free enough to touch him, to kiss him, he'd know she wasn't afraid of him any longer, that she was beginning to trust him.

Approaching him slowly, Alicia stood close to his chair. He saw the last remnants of anger leave her expression as well as a flash of apprehension in her eyes. Sensing her desire to reach out to him was as real as the scent of her delicate perfume, he waited... and hoped.

Her hand came toward him, and he could see it was trembling. Wanting to take it, he knew he shouldn't. He had to let her do this. Her fingers felt like the quick but fluttering graze of a butterfly's wings. On their second pass down his cheek, they were more like the brush of satin. His body stirred, tensed, readied him for more.

She leaned toward him and stroked his jaw, then she took a deep breath and dropped her hand to her side.

He opened his arms to her and said, "Come here." Pulling her gently onto his lap, he held her close. "That wasn't so hard, was it?"

She shook her head as she leaned against his chest. "Doug's an old friend, Jon. You're . . . different. When I touch you, there's more than friendship. There's heat and fire and excitement and it scares me."

Her honesty touched him, excited him, brought a blaze of fire to his loins. "Why does it scare you?" he asked, his voice coming out in a husky murmur.

She played with a button on his shirt. "Because I've never felt it before. Because it muddles my thinking and seems to turn the world upside down."

"I'm glad the feeling's mutual." He gently tipped her chin up and took her lips with a need that left them both breathless.

Keeping her secure in his hold, he said, "I'm going to miss you."

She pushed away and sat up as well as she could within his arms. "You're going back to California?"

"Not yet. I have to go to Minneapolis. I'm leaving to-morrow morning."

"But Emily's graduation ceremony is Wednesday evening."

"I know. I'm going to have to miss it. I'll talk to her about it later."

Alicia went rigid on his lap and pulled away from his arms. Standing, she went to the window above the sink and stared into the backyard. The yellow gingham curtains fluttered against the windowsill.

He could imagine what she was thinking. But she had to understand his position. "Alicia, this trip can't be helped. I have a newspaper whose employees are on the verge of a walkout. I probably should have flown out before now, but I was hoping the situation would resolve itself."

She didn't turn around. "Emily only graduates from kindergarten once."

"For heaven's sake, it's an hour-long ceremony." He pushed away his coffee mug. "She'll forget about it a few minutes after it's over."

Alicia swung around and faced him. "Will she? Will she forget you weren't there?"

"I don't need a guilt trip," he said, standing and pushing in his chair.

"That's what parenthood's all about, Jon. Making the right choices at the right times. Often guilt goes along with it."

"Don't make this into something that proves whether or not I'm a good father. I've been here almost daily for the last seven weeks..."

"I know you have." She didn't say it sarcastically or with an angry inflection.

He felt as if more than the table's width separated them. "But you don't think that's enough."

She lifted her gaze to his. "You have to decide what's enough. You've missed five years of Emily's life. Her first smile, her first tooth, her first step. Do you want to miss her first academic achievement, too?"

"It's a kindergarten graduation, Alicia, not the Nobel prize."

Alicia placed her hands on the chair. "How do you decide what's important, Jon? What might not be important to you, could be important to her. What if this were her high school graduation?"

He didn't like where this was headed or the defensiveness he felt with Alicia's probing questions. "I'd still have to go."

Her brow creased with her frown. "And you think Emily wouldn't remember that?"

"Emily is going to have to face the realities of life just like everyone else."

"Is that the reality where her father puts her second behind his business concerns?"

Jon shoved his hands into his pockets, old memories niggling at him—memories of his father missing his sports events, his own high school graduation. Instead of focusing on that, he focused on the problem. "I'm dealing with a possible strike. It affects almost a hundred workers, let alone setting a precedent with my other papers. I can't take care of this long distance."

She lifted her hand in a resigned gesture. "So... fine. Go. We'll see you when you get back."

He took a step toward her. "Alicia..."

"What do you want me to say, Jon?"

That was easy. "I want you to say you understand."

Her voice softened, but her disappointment was evident. "I understand that you don't yet realize how comprehensive being a father is, or how much Emily needs you."

He felt he was losing ground fast. If Alicia had shown anger, he could have fought it. But her protective feelings for their daughter weren't something he could fault her for. "It's different being a father than a mother. What I accomplish in business now will be Emily's someday. I need to safeguard it."

Alicia shook her head. "That's the propaganda men have been using as an excuse for years. Believe it if you want to, but don't try to feed it to me. You go, Jon. You take care of business."

Her words rankled. Probably because they contained an element of truth. He didn't want to look at any of it too carefully. "I'll be back this evening to say goodbye to Emily."

"Fine."

But it wasn't fine. He didn't like the way he felt torn in two. It was part of parenthood he'd never anticipated.

Alicia received the phone call from her lawyer the next day. Jon was Emily's father. The lab had taken the testing to 99.9 percent accuracy level. And Alicia had no doubt about that last probability of uncertainty. She looked at Emily and she saw Jon. She looked at Jon and saw Emily. Their head movements, a certain expression, their eyes...

Her acceptance had happened slowly over the past seven weeks. So had falling in love. She was in love with Jonathan Wescott, her daughter's father, and didn't know what to do about it. She was so afraid loving Jon meant losing herself.

He'd explained to Emily he wouldn't be able to come to her graduation. She'd taken in everything he'd said. She'd nodded, her eyes big and wide as he asked if she understood. But it wasn't until Alicia was alone with her daughter at bedtime that tears came to Emily's eyes and she'd confided to her mother she wanted Jon to be there.

Alicia had held her daughter and stroked her hair, just letting her be sad, not trying to explain or excuse. She was disappointed with Jon for leaving, but she knew he had to learn how to father, to come to terms with the difference a child would make in his life. Jon was a loving, compassionate man who was terrific with Emily. But he wasn't used to living for and caring for someone else.

Alicia wondered if Jon's lawyer had called him with the news or was waiting until he returned.

Later in the evening, when she picked up the phone and heard Jon's voice on the other end, she suddenly hesitated to ask. If he didn't know, she was seized by the desire to keep Emily hers for just a little while longer.

"Hi, Alicia. How are you?"

"I'm fine."

"Are you still angry?"

She hesitated. "I was more disappointed than angry."

"I see."

She broke the silence. "Do you want to speak to Emily?"

"Yes, that's why I called. I want her to know I haven't forgotten about her."

"Hold on a minute." Alicia called for Emily.

Jon rubbed the back of his neck. He hadn't cared if anyone was disappointed in him since his father was living.

"Mr. Wescott! Are you in Minnie-aplis?" Emily asked.

"I sure am, honey. Are you ready for tomorrow night?"

"Mommy bought me a new dress. I wish you could see it."

"I'll see it when I get back."

"No, I mean when I wear my hat and go on the stage."

It might not have been clear to him before, but it was apparent to him now that his daughter didn't understand why he couldn't be at her graduation. So much for explaining logically to a five-year-old. "Your mom said she'll take pictures. So I will see you, just not tomorrow night."

Her voice was very disappointed. "Okay."

Jon tried to fix her unhappiness the only way he knew how. "I can bring you something from Minneapolis. A new doll, a new game."

"Nah. I just wish you could come back. D'you want Mommy now?"

Jon assured Emily he did. But the rest of his conversation with Alicia wasn't much more than goodbye. He stared at the phone long after he hung it up in the editor in chief's office. He had ninety employees at this newspaper who had finally agreed to talk instead of strike. But they had so much to negotiate. It wasn't just the raise, but health care benefits, too. And he couldn't be in two places at one time. Just what the hell was he supposed to do?

Emily waved from the stage. Alicia and Ria waved back and grinned at each other.

Ria commented, "She's really enjoying the limelight. You can tell some of those kids don't want to be up there."

"I had to brush her hair three times before she was satisfied. Do you think that's a sign she cares too much about how she looks?"

"It's a sign she's a female. No man would care how his hair looked under a hat."

Alicia laughed until she looked toward the aisle and saw a tall man in a dark suit striding toward her row. Jon excused himself to the two people sitting at the end and slid past three empty seats to sit next to Alicia.

"You can close your mouth now." He leaned past Alicia and said, "Hi, Ria."

"Better late than never," her twin quipped with a grin.

"That's what I thought but I don't know if your sister will agree."

"I'm glad you're here," Alicia murmured, trying to keep her heart from leaping from her chest.

He covered her hand with his. "Miss me?"

Instead of answering, knowing she'd missed him too much, she asked, "How did you get away? Is everything settled?"

"No. But I brought in reinforcements. My right-hand man from L.A. flew in this morning. If he runs into trouble, I might have to fly out again tomorrow. But for tonight, I'm here. You were right. I have to learn to judge when Emily needs to come before business. After talking to Emily on the phone, I realized she needed my presence not my presents. That's what you've been trying to tell me all along."

Her heart swelled with love for him. She no longer wanted to keep the blood-test results to herself. "Jon, my lawyer called me. You're Emily's father."

"I know. I had a message from my lawyer."

Alicia had to be honest with him. "I knew last night when I talked to you, but..."

"You wanted to hold onto Emily a little longer."

He understood her so well, too well sometimes. Lifting her hand, he brought her fingers to his lips and kissed her knuckles. The erotic sensation of his lips nuzzling her fingers shortened her breath and raised the temperature in the auditorium at least ten degrees.

Suddenly Emily saw him in the audience. She smiled and waved so vigorously her mortarboard almost fell from her head.

Jon waved back, then leaned close to Alicia, his breath warming her cheek. "Are we going to celebrate with hot fudge sundaes?"

Alicia's stomach quivered, her heart tripped, and she couldn't find her voice for a moment. Finally she managed, "Maybe even a banana split."

He chuckled, then leaned away. She knew her heart was gone and it would be almost impossible to snatch it back.

After the graduation ceremony, Ria took photographs and joined them for ice cream at the family restaurant they frequented for broasted chicken. She finished her last spoonful of ice cream and patted her stomach. "That's my treat for the week. Back to turkey burgers and sprouts tomorrow."

"Before or after you skydive?" Alicia asked.

"Skydiving?" Jon asked. "I've tried hang gliding but never skydiving."

Ria took her wallet from her purse. "I took it up to combat stress. It takes me above problems that seem too large to handle."

Skydiving wasn't something Alicia would ever want to try, but Ria had always been a lot more adventurous. So Alicia swallowed her own fears when Ria talked about the sensation of falling to earth, and tried to understand her twin's excitement.

Ria stood and Jon insisted on paying her part of the bill. Finally giving in, she patted him on the shoulder. "I'm glad you made it back." She kissed Emily, hugged Alicia and left the three of them alone.

Only one other table was still occupied by customers. The waitress had gone to the counter at the back of the restaurant. Jon looked at Alicia and said quietly, "What do you think about telling her now?"

Alicia knew immediately what he was talking about. "This is a special night. I think it's a good idea."

Emily was concentrating on scooping up the last bit of chocolate fudge floating on her melted ice cream.

Jon crossed his arms on the table in front of him. "Emily?"

Alicia thought he looked a bit nervous. That was unusual for him. The idea of Jon being vulnerable endeared him to her even more. She took her napkin and wiped her daughter's mouth. "Mr. Wescott has something he'd like to tell you."

The five-year-old gave Jon all her attention.

"Do you remember when we had the doctor take our blood?"

She nodded solemnly.

"Well, the people at the lab did some special tests on it, and your blood and my blood match." His voice lowered and became slightly husky. "That means I'm your dad."

Emily looked to her mother.

"Honey, you know you're very special, that the man you don't remember very well and I adopted you just after you were born. Jon is your real dad."

Emily looked confused for a few moments and Alicia waited for the questions she knew would come. "You mean I have a dad now like my friends?"

"You definitely have a dad now," Jon assured her.

"Are you gonna live with us?"

Jon stared at Alicia for a long moment. "No. And soon I have to go back to where I live. Would you like to come visit?"

"With Mommy?"

"Yes. We can take a plane through the clouds. How does that sound?" he asked.

"Up in the sky?"

"Yep."

She thought about it. "As long as Mommy comes it's okay. Can Aunt Ria come, too?"

Alicia stroked Emily's hair, knowing her daughter was trying to sort it all out. "No. Just us and . . . your dad." It seemed unusual to actually call Jon that.

Suddenly the full impact of what Jon and Alicia had told Emily appeared to hit her. She grinned and asked, "Can I call you Daddy?"

The question seemed to take Jon by surprise. He swallowed hard and cleared his throat before he said, "I'd like that very much."

Alicia thought she saw his eyes glisten, and she realized how much Emily meant to him, how he'd wanted this moment since the day he'd appeared at her door. She was thankful for the happiness on Emily's face, the satisfaction and love in Jon's eyes. But the question Alicia had to ask herself was whether Jon had feelings for her as well as Emily. If she weren't Emily's mother, would he want her in his life?

Alicia teed up as Jon had showed her on the first four holes. She tried to remember everything he'd told her. Never having played golf before today, she still felt awkward. Rocking back and forth to feel her balance, she planted her feet. Bringing up the club, she followed through as best she could. But she hacked the ball. It rolled about three yards and stopped.

She looked at it and shook her head. "I don't know, Jon. I don't think this is my game. My form must be all wrong."

"There's nothing wrong with your form," Jon responded, looking her up and down with obvious appreciation. She'd chosen the turquoise flowered culottes and matching blouse with care and now was glad she had.

He'd convinced her to let Gertie baby-sit so she could take the afternoon off and go with him to pick up their airplane tickets for next week, to play a game of golf, then go to dinner and a movie with him later. She was looking forward to it, though she didn't know what would happen after the movie, after they returned home and the baby-sitter left. Each time they kissed, she could feel Jon's restraint. She didn't know how much longer he'd pull away without wanting fulfillment. She didn't know how much longer she'd deny them both. Yet could she make love with him without knowing how he felt about her?

"Can you tell me what I'm doing wrong?" she asked, trying to keep her mind on the game, rather than on Jon's muscular legs, tan against his white shorts and the black wisps of hair at the neck of his yellow polo shirt.

He stepped behind her and put his hands on top of hers on the club. "Your grip is fine. You caught onto that quickly. What you need to remember is to keep the movement in your upper body." He swung the club for her, his chest pressed against her back.

His thighs against her buttocks felt intimate and erotic. How was she supposed to keep her thoughts on her swing?

"Your body should turn toward your target."

Her target right now was holding onto her sanity while he pressed against her. "Jon..." Her voice was a squeak. She tried again. "Jon, I think I've got it now."

"I know *I* have," he murmured into her ear. He straightened, turned her around and slid his hands under her hair, anchoring her head. His lips sought hers.

The kiss devoured her. Jon's tongue mated with hers until she wanted the same union for their bodies. When he tore his lips away, she moaned in protest.

He tilted his forehead against hers. "I want to make love to you."

She slipped her hands away from the back of his neck and braced them on his chest. "I don't know if I'm ready. I don't know—" Suddenly a sharp pain shot through Alicia's arm and the fear that gripped her made her queasy. She knew something was terribly wrong... with Ria.

Jon lifted his head. "Ready for what? You want me, I want you. Nothing could be simpler."

Shivering, she pushed away from him and wrapped her arms around herself. "We have to go back to the clubhouse."

Jon let her go and stared at her, perplexed. "Why? Because I told you I want to make love to you?"

"No. I have to call Ria."

"Ria's skydiving."

"No. She's in trouble. Something happened. I can feel it."

"Alicia..."

"Don't try to analyze it, Jon. This happens between us. It's not logical. It's a bond. Something's wrong and I have to get to her."

He studied Alicia carefully for a moment. "All right. Let's go. But if this is your way of evading a discussion you don't want to have—"

"Jon!"

"I'm sorry. I shouldn't have said that. Let's go and find out what this is all about." He picked up the golf bag while she retrieved the club that had fallen to the grass when they'd kissed.

As they rode back to the clubhouse in the golf cart, she ran her fingers over the dull ache in her arm and prayed.

Chapter Eight

Jon kept his hand at the small of Alicia's back as they hurried down the hospital corridor. The message at the clubhouse had made Alicia go pale, and when she'd followed its directive to call the hospital and her hands had begun trembling, he was afraid she'd faint. But as she'd told him before, she was not as delicate as she looked.

The nurse hadn't told her much, just that Ria was in "satisfactory" condition and having tests run. When they arrived at the emergency room, Alicia was informed that the doctor had admitted Ria and she would be settled in room 543 after the tests. They could wait in the fifth floor lounge.

It seemed Alicia wasn't any better at waiting than Jon was, at least not where her twin's health was concerned. As she paced across the lounge, she peeked up the hall. "At least they could tell me what the tests are for. I'm her sister!"

"The doctor has to give you that information," he soothed.

"Then where is he?" she asked, her voice rising.

Jon stood and crossed to her. Wrapping his arms around her, he held on tight. When she sank against him, he tightened his hold. Her heart was beating fast, and he knew it was from worry.

She raised her head, tears running down her cheek. "If anything happens to her..."

Jon hadn't truly realized until now the bond between these two sisters. They were more than close. "She'll be all right. They wouldn't list her as satisfactory..."

"Mrs. Fallon?"

Jon kept his arm around Alicia's waist as she turned toward the voice. A middle-aged doctor dressed in green scrubs came toward them.

"Yes, I'm Mrs. Fallon. How's Ria?"

He rubbed his hand across his forehead. "Giving me a rough time. She wouldn't take anything to relax her before we set her arm. The CT scan doesn't show any brain injury but I want to keep her for observation overnight."

"What happened?" Jon asked, giving Alicia time to absorb the information.

Hearing commotion in the hall, the doctor turned toward it. "I'm sure she'd rather tell you herself. Try to convince her to stay in bed so we don't have to tie her down, okay?"

As the doctor left, Alicia mumbled something under her breath about some people not using the good sense God gave them and started toward room 543.

Jon bit back a chuckle and followed her. If Ria was giving the staff grief, she was on the mend already. Her recovery was bound to be a battle of wills.

Ria was settled into bed when they arrived at the room. Her blond hair was matted and pushed behind her ears. She looked pale and strained, but she smiled when Alicia approached the bed. "Hi, sis. Guess I did it, didn't I?"

Alicia sat on the bed and held Ria for a long but careful hug. When she leaned back, some of the worry on her face had eased. "What did you do?"

Ria settled her cast on the bed beside her. "I'm not sure exactly. I don't know if my attention wandered for a moment . . . or if I got caught up in the excitement. But I wasn't ready for the landing. Isn't that stupid?"

"No, it's dangerous," Alicia scolded, taking her sister's hand. "What am I going to do with you?"

Ria shrugged and winced. "I don't know. Lock me in my apartment, I guess."

"As if you wouldn't pick the lock," Jon said with a smile.

Ria shook her finger at him. "You got my number way too fast, Jonathan Wescott." Suddenly she closed her eyes for a moment.

"What's wrong?" Alicia asked, her expression anxious again.

"Just a headache. That's why they're keeping me here. Thank goodness for helmets or . . ."

Alicia whispered, "Don't say it."

Jon squeezed her shoulder, and she covered his hand with hers.

Ria noticed the gesture and smiled. "I guess you two will be off to L.A. soon."

Alicia shifted on the bed. "We were supposed to go next week. But now, you can't be alone. With a concussion . . ."

"Don't be silly," Ria protested. "I'm fine. I . . ." She closed her eyes again.

Alicia frowned. "Sure. You're just fine. You need someone to take care of you."

Ria muttered through pursed lips, "I do not."

Jon intervened. "Why don't we put off that discussion until later. Is there anything you need?"

She looked down at the hospital gown. "Yes, a decent nightgown and robe, toothbrush and toothpaste, maybe slippers. And could you feed Merlina and Lancelot and play with them a little? They're going to miss me being around. And there are plants in the kitchen that need water."

"Merlina and Lancelot?" Jon checked with Alicia.

Her reluctant smile was rueful. "They're Ria's cats. They're declawed and stay indoors. I can stop at your apartment before I come in for visiting hours tonight."

"You were supposed to go out to dinner," Ria reminded.

Jon quickly said, "We can do that another time. Alicia won't have a good time if she's worrying about you."

Ria disagreed. "But she has to eat. Take her someplace and force-feed her if you have to."

Alicia remembered Ria's words later that evening as they stopped at her sister's apartment after a quick dinner. Jon didn't have to force-feed her, but she'd barely picked at her food. He seemed to understand and had held her hand throughout most of the meal.

Using her key, Alicia let them inside the first-floor living space. A southwest theme prevailed with the turquoise and peach and earth tones on the fabric of the sofa and chair.

Two cats entered the living room from a hall that led to Ria's bedroom. Alicia scooped up the fat yellow tabby. "How are you doing Lancelot?" She scratched behind his ear and he purred.

The other cat, a silver longhair wrapped around Jon's legs. "And this is Merlina, I presume?"

Alicia laughed. "Ria had to use a doll bottle to feed her when she got her because she was so small. And she named the kitten Merlin because she thought it was a male. A few weeks later, she revised the name."

Jon chuckled and headed for the kitchen. "Where's the cat food?"

"Kitchen closet. Third shelf. Give them one of the small cans. I'll pack Ria's overnight bag."

"And the watering can?" he called over his shoulder.

"Under the sink," she called back with a smile.

Alicia had insisted Jon didn't have to come along to the hospital again, but he'd said he wanted to. His support felt good. Right. Just like his arms and the taste of his kiss.

When she reentered the living room, she plopped the overnight case by the door. Jon was sitting on the sofa leafing through a magazine, Merlina curled up beside him.

He put the magazine in the rack where he'd found it. "Ready?"

"Mmm-hmm. Except...I want to tell you how sorry I am I can't fly back to L.A. with you Thursday. I was looking forward to it."

He patted Merlina's head and stood. Lancelot jumped up beside the gray cat. "Yes, you can. I've taken care of everything."

His words warned her of trouble, although his expression was relaxed. He'd disappeared for a while as she visited with Ria. As she changed clothes at home afterward, he'd told her he had to make some calls. She'd assumed they were business calls. "What do you mean you've taken care of everything?"

"I know you're concerned about Ria. So I found a private duty nurse that will move in with her and take care of her when she comes home from the hospital. That way you don't have to worry, and we can still fly out on Thursday."

Alicia's heart beat faster. Fury boiled up and spilled over. "And you felt no need to discuss this with me first?"

He flicked his hand. "I didn't want you to have to be concerned with details."

"What you wanted was to keep your plans unchanged. My sister is *not* a detail. I love her. I'd postpone a hundred trips for her. You have no right trying to run my life!"

"I'm doing no such thing. I'm trying to make it easier."

She pushed her hair behind her ear and fixed him with a protesting stare. "You're trying to make it easier for yourself. It's your way or no way. I had a father like that. As a child, I had no choice. He backed me into a corner and I had to stay there. But I'm an adult now and I make my own decisions. What's easier for you might not be easier for me. All you want to do is get me to California."

"And what's wrong with that?" he asked impatiently. "You just said you were looking forward to it."

"But not when Ria needs me."

He arched his dark brows and asked none too gently, "What if *I* need you? My life is upside down with my daughter living three thousand miles away. We need to make decisions now before Emily and I have to spend any more time apart. Can't you understand that?''

Understanding his frustration, she offered, ''Jon, I'm only talking about postponing the trip a few weeks.''

''Are you?'' His eyes narrowed, his posture straightened.

If he was accusing her of something, she wished he'd just say it. ''I don't know what you mean.''

He pinned her to the spot with green eyes that were hard. His voice was rough. ''I'm not your father, Alicia. Since the moment we met you've had no trouble standing up to me. Just because I'm trying to do something to help you doesn't mean I'm trying to run your life.''

She felt as if she was the one who had done something wrong, and she hadn't. ''It feels like it.''

He studied her long and speculatively until she felt as if she were a specimen under a microscope.

''What?'' she asked when she couldn't stand his perusal a moment longer.

There was an unnatural immobility about him, a stoic objectiveness that gave her chills. ''I don't think you know what an equal man-woman relationship is. Patrick Fallon was a kind father figure who gave you everything you wanted, who let you do whatever you wanted.''

''He respected me. He—''

Not letting her finish, he cut in harshly, ''How was the sex, Alicia? Was there passion between you? Did you burst into flames for him when he kissed you as you do with me?''

Heat flushed her cheeks. ''This has nothing to do with sex.''

Jon took a step closer, and she could feel the sensual sizzle that always vibrated between them. ''What happens in the bedroom is a good gauge of what happens in the rest of the marriage. Your childhood set you up for the relationship you had with Patrick. A nice, easy, comfortable companionship. Don't you want more than that?''

She was too filled with hurt and anger at that moment to want anything except for Jon to leave. ''I want to make my own decisions. I want to live my own life.''

''You have to consider Emily, too.''

That comment hurt even more than the rest. ''I always consider Emily. And if you don't know that by now, you don't know me at all.'' She bit her lip and tried to hold back her tears.

''Alicia . . .''

She couldn't listen to any more of his criticism, or battle against his commanding presence. ''I think you'd better leave. I'll use Ria's car to go to the hospital.''

His jaw set, his face grew expressionless, his gaze became shuttered so she couldn't see his thoughts or his feelings as he answered, ''If that's what you prefer.''

She didn't know what she preferred. She felt as if she'd lost something precious; she felt as if Jon was already three thousand miles away.

Silence stretched between them until Jon challenged, ''I'll wait to hear from you. But I'm going to be on that plane Thursday. I've been away too long already.'' He didn't wait for a response, but strode out the door and didn't look back.

Alicia put a fresh glass of orange juice on the table next to Ria's chair. ''Need anything else?''

Ria stood and started up the short flight of stairs.

''Where are you going?''

''To the bathroom if you don't mind.''

Alicia sighed and sat on the sofa. ''What's wrong?''

Ria shook her head slowly and gave her sister a wry smile. "I've been here two days and you're driving me nuts." Before Alicia could feel hurt, she went on, "You know I love you, sis, and normally I love spending time with you, but you're hovering. I can't take a breath without you asking me if I'm okay. I think there's more wrong with you than with me."

Alicia took one of those deep breaths that she'd been taking many of in the past three days. "There's nothing wrong with me."

Ria came back into the room and sat next to her twin. "Call Jon."

"No!"

"Why not?"

"Because I don't know what to say to him or how to act. He said some things...that might be true." Alicia averted her eyes. "Patrick and I had a good marriage, didn't we?"

Ria shrugged. "That depends on what you mean by good."

She faced Ria squarely. "We were friends, for goodness sake. Isn't that important?"

"Are you and Jon friends?"

Alicia got up and paced to the picture window. "That's different."

"There's something more with Jon, isn't there?"

"There's so much with Jon. It overwhelms me sometimes. He's so forceful, so confident, so...sexy."

"Sis, the absence of conflict doesn't mean you had a good marriage with Patrick, it doesn't mean it was not good. Personally, Patrick was too bland for my taste. But I'm different than you."

"Jon thinks I'm using your accident to postpone going to L.A."

"Are you?"

"Oh, I don't know. Sure, I'm going to have to make major decisions, and I don't know if I'm ready for that, but I care about you."

"I know that," Ria said softly. "What are you afraid of most?"

"Of caring for Jon a lot more than he cares for me. I'm not sure what exactly he wants. I'm afraid if he feels anything for me, it's tied up with what he feels for Emily."

"You both need some time."

Alicia spun away from the picture window to face her twin. "I guess that's part of the problem. I don't feel like I have it. When I go to California, I'll be in his world. I don't know if I'm ready to live in it permanently. Lord, I'd miss you."

"There are airplanes."

Alicia shook her head. "Our phone bills would be astronomical."

Ria stood and went to Alicia. "You're jumping the gun. You're just going for a visit. Or are you afraid Jon will steamroll over what you want?"

The answer came immediately. "Yes."

"You're stronger than that."

"Not where Emily is concerned. I have to do what's best for her."

"You'll figure it out."

Jon was wary as he stepped up to Alicia's front door. She hadn't called him; Ria had. She'd said she wanted to talk to him. Giving Alicia and himself time had been damn hard. Not seeing Emily had been just as hard. He wasn't being stubborn. He'd just hoped Alicia would call him, say the trip was still on . . .

When he rang the bell, he didn't know what to expect.

Alicia answered the door and couldn't have looked more shocked. Her blue eyes widened and her cheeks grew rosy.

"You didn't know I was coming, did you?" he asked.

"Come on in, Jon," Ria called from inside.

Alicia gave her sister a sharp look and backed up so he could step in. "What's going on, Ria?"

Ria looked a hundred percent better than the last time he'd seen her. Color was back in her face, her hair fell straight and soft along her cheeks. Dressed in hot pink shorts and T-shirt, she looked healthy except for the cast on her arm.

Ria motioned Jon toward the sofa. "Sit down. Both of you. I have something to say."

"Uh-oh," Alicia mumbled.

If the situation wasn't so awkward, Jon might have smiled. He sat at one end of the sofa; Alicia sat at the other.

Ria looked from one to the other and shook her head. "All right. This is what I've decided. I do not need a private duty nurse, though, Jon, I do appreciate your generous offer. It was generous, wasn't it, Alicia?"

"I suppose," her sister admitted grudgingly.

"It would be a waste of your money and I can't stand baby-sitters. Which brings me to my next point. Alicia is pampering me to death and it better stop or I'll get used to it and need a maid and butler. We all know I can't afford that. So I'm going home tonight. One or both of you can have the pleasure of chauffeuring me since I can't drive until I see the doctor on Friday."

"You can't be alone," Alicia protested. "What about the headaches?"

"The headaches are infrequent now. There's no reason I can't be alone." Before Alicia could interrupt, she went on. "But since I know you'll worry, and since you'll be leaving for L.A. on Thursday, I've asked Gertie if she'll come in during the day while you're gone. Will that satisfy you?"

"I don't know if I'm going to L.A." Alicia stubbornly kept her gaze away from Jon's.

"Yes, and that's point number three. I'm going out on the patio to have a tea party with Emily. She's all set up and waiting for me. You two may join us if and when you straighten out your differences. Got it?"

Jon wasn't any happier with Ria's maneuvering than Alicia. "And you think this manipulation is going to work?"

Ria stood and walked to the archway of the kitchen. "I don't know. I hope so. Because if you're in the same shape as my sister, I don't see how you're getting anything done, either." She took a few steps and called back, "Emily and I will be waiting."

Jon turned toward Alicia. She looked at him for a moment, then looked down into her lap. "I didn't know what she'd planned. If I had . . ."

"You would have warned me."

"Something like that," she murmured.

"I was hoping you'd call."

"I was hoping *you'd* call." She shot back the words.

"And apologize for being high-handed?" he asked, deciding the first step wasn't so hard to take.

"No, so I could tell you that some of what you said was true," she answered with a soft sigh. "*Most* of what you said was true."

He moved closer to her. "I had no right to judge your marriage."

She gazed into his eyes then, and he had to catch his breath because she appeared totally vulnerable and open to him. "My father controlled our household. He wielded all the power. I didn't think I'd ever marry. I had no desire to be under someone's foot all my life. But then I met Patrick. He was everything my father wasn't— kind, gentle, understanding. He didn't demand anything. He just gave. And I gave back whatever I could. I loved keeping our house looking nice, I loved cooking for him, and after we adopted Emily, I loved caring for her. We were friends, Jon. And I'll never be sorry I married him."

Jon couldn't help the jealousy that twisted his gut, but he said, "I'm sorry I said what I did."

Alicia shook her head. "I'm not. Because in a way, you were right. Patrick was the perfect father figure. And I guess I loved him because of it. He never once made me feel inferior, or unimportant. He made me feel proud to be who I was. But there wasn't much passion. When he kissed me, I never felt what I feel with you."

Jon put his arm along the back of the sofa, not quite touching her. "I'm a take-charge kind of person, Alicia. I'm that way in business, and I guess I can't become someone else in my personal life. Women I've known in the past never complained, but then, maybe I was never involved with them the way I'm involved with you. And Emily."

"Not even Cecile?"

Could she be jealous, too? He smiled. "When I think about it now, I can't imagine being married to Cecile. She was stiff and brittle—compared to you. The idea of her being Emily's mother..." He shook his head. "I can't picture it."

A small smile played on Alicia's lips. "You know if you had called to see Emily, I wouldn't have kept you from her. I never will. She missed you. She asked me about you every day."

"It's only been three days. I thought we both could use some time to think. You know, if you come to L.A., it's only a visit. You don't have to make any decisions until you're ready."

Her expression was skeptical. "You don't think you're going to push just a little?"

He moved his hand to her shoulder and played with the tips of her hair. "Maybe a little." Sliding his hand under her hair, he caressed her nape. "You said Emily missed me. What about you?"

She reached up and stroked the hair that fell across his brow. "I missed you, too."

It was what he'd been waiting to hear, all he needed to hear. Except for getting Alicia to accept his invitation to California. "Will you fly to L.A. with me on Thursday?"

"I certainly can't disappoint Ria after she's made all these arrangements, can I?"

He tweaked her nose. "She is a rare bird."

"She's special."

He leaned toward her and nudged Alicia's face toward his. "So are you." Sliding his tongue along her bottom lip, he laved it until she separated her lips. When she did, he didn't enter, but nibbled gently.

Her arms went around his neck.

Scooping her onto his lap, he teased her with his mouth, until finally her tongue touched his upper lip. Alicia was setting herself free, little by little, touch by touch, stroke by stroke. What would she be like when she trusted herself and she trusted him enough to respond without thinking, without holding back? Just a taste of her made him aroused enough that he hurt. Would she let him make love to her in California? On a deserted beach? In his home? In his bed?

He wanted to discover everything she had to give, everything she was. Giving her the passion she deserved ranked right up there with making his home hers and Emily's, too. Would she live with him? Or would she insist on a separate residence? Unless ...

They could get married. They could give Emily the home she needed.

He kissed Alicia with a vehemence he'd never remembered experiencing. Her whimper increased his hunger, heated his blood, aroused him until he knew she could feel him under her. Her hands delved into his hair. Her tongue chased his, tempted, teased. She was all woman— hot, and soft, and responsive in his arms. Kissing wasn't enough. It was only the beginning.

He crushed her to him, hoping he wasn't scaring her, part of him not caring. Her moan didn't sound like fear. When he tore his lips from hers to kiss her neck, her low, murmured, "Jon" sounded more like a plea. Her yellow cotton top wasn't much of a barrier, yet was too much. Closing his hand over her breast, he sighed with the sheer pleasure of touching her intimately. She arched beneath him, rubbing against him, creating a need so strong he was afraid he'd explode.

Lifting the edge of her top, he found the warm skin of her midriff. She couldn't have been any silkier, any more alluring, any more a dream he'd had over and over since they'd met. Desire throbbed as an aching yearning almost to the point of pain.

Alicia lost all her hesitancy, all her doubts, all her wondering about whether loving Jon could turn out to be a mistake for her... and Emily. Jon excited her, aroused her, lifted her out of her ordinary life making each moment they spent together extraordinary. He was strong, and compassionate, and understanding, and she loved him so.

As he touched her breast, light shattered into thousands of shards, piercing her, tingling in so many places she couldn't decide what she wanted him to touch first. This was passion. This was need. This was making love.

Suddenly Jon took his hand away. He nuzzled her shoulder with his chin and said hoarsely, "We've got to stop. Ria and Emily are right outside."

She should feel embarrassed, getting carried away like this, forgetting where she was. But she didn't feel embarrassed, she felt incomplete, unsatisfied. As she lay against Jon's chest, counting the beats of his heart, the question she'd been shoving aside burst clear.

She'd been making love. But did Jon love her? Did he think of her as more than Emily's mother? Did he feel more than desire? And what would happen *after* her visit to California?

Chapter Nine

The house overlooking the beach suited Jon perfectly. It was one floor, sprawling, with lots of windows facing the ocean. It was one of those dream houses that everyone who loved the shore imagined owning. Alicia couldn't believe she'd be spending two weeks here.

Jon pulled his BMW into the garage. One of his employees had delivered it to the airport. That in itself had given Alicia an idea of the service he was used to. Their worlds were so different.

A white luxury sedan sat in the driveway, and passing it made Alicia nervous because she suspected who owned it.

Jon confirmed her guess when he opened her car door. "Mom's here. When I called her last night, she said she couldn't wait to meet you and she'd bring in a light supper so we didn't have to worry about cooking."

"She didn't have to go to all that trouble."

He smiled and shrugged. "That's Mom."

Emily had fallen asleep in the car on the way to Jon's house from the airport. Alicia opened the back door, kissed her daughter's forehead and smoothed her hand over Emily's brow. "We're here, honey."

"At Daddy's?"

Every time Emily used the new title, Alicia smiled. "Yes, ma'am. And there's somebody Daddy wants you to meet."

Jon reached in and lifted Emily into his arms, nodding to the trunk. "I'll get the luggage later."

The garage led into a breezeway, which led into the kitchen. Granite counters topped by pale gray cabinets gave the room a soothing air. Jon strode through it and Alicia only caught a quick look. The dining room was a melody of glass—a glass table, a glass hutch that took up one wall, a glass-and-chrome modern, multilayered chandelier. It wasn't a room for a child.

The large picture window in the living room provided a magnificent view of the ocean. Gray-blue waves rushed and splashed into crests of white foam. The wide expanse of shoreline seemed part of the living room. The sea green leather couch and chairs were an echo of the tranquillity the rest of the house projected.

A petite woman in designer jeans and yellow silk blouse sat on the sofa with a kind smile on her face. Her hair was as dark as Jon's though streaked with gray, softly curled and professionally coiffed around her face.

She stood as Jon approached her with Emily in his arms. Her gaze met Alicia's for a moment, then she made the little girl her focus. "Hello, there, Emily."

Emily pushed her finger into her mouth and kept her head on Jon's shoulder.

Jon patted Emily's back. "Honey, this is your grandmother."

"I already have one."

Alicia could feel Mrs. Wescott's disappointment. Going to her daughter, Alicia held out her arms and took her from Jon. "Now you have two. This is your dad's mommy." She set Emily on the floor.

Mrs. Wescott sent Alicia a grateful smile and crouched down in front of her granddaughter. "Would you like a snack or would you like to see your playroom?"

Emily's face broke into a grin. "The playroom."

Jon's mother held out her hand to the little girl. "C'mon. It's right over here." She pointed to a room down the hall.

Emily looked to her mother. Alicia nodded. "Go ahead. I'll get us a snack."

Mrs. Wescott said, "There are carrot and celery sticks in the refrigerator. And I bought some oatmeal cookies." Guiding Emily into the playroom, she said to her, "Your dad told me you like lollipops. Which flavor's your favorite?"

As their voices faded into the hall, Jon said, "Mom's not ignoring you, you know."

"I know. She wants to get to know her granddaughter. There's no etiquette book for this situation." But Alicia wondered what judgment Marilyn Wescott had made about her at first sight. It was amazing how much she wanted the woman to like her. She shouldn't care, but she did.

Jon put his arm around her shoulders. He gave her a kiss made erotic by quick exploring strokes of his tongue. It knocked everything else out of her head until he broke away. "Unfortunately this isn't the time or the place. Let's get those carrot sticks."

A short time later, Emily came running into the kitchen dragging a teddy bear, almost as large as she was, by his ear. "Look what Grandma gave me!"

"I see. He's an armful."

"And I have paints, and crayons and games. You gotta see."

Mrs. Wescott had followed her granddaughter more sedately. "I'll have you know that roomful was Jon's idea. I wouldn't have bought quite as much."

Alicia shook her head at him, but he just shrugged.

He said to Emily, "Grab some carrot sticks, kiddo, and you and I can go walk on the beach."

Alicia knew what he was doing. He wanted Emily to feel at home, he wanted her to feel she belonged. He also wanted Alicia to get to know his mother. Part of her was glad; the other part was apprehensive.

After he and Emily left, she turned to Marilyn. "Thank you for the supper in the refrigerator," she said. "And the groceries. You really didn't have to do that."

"I wanted to." Marilyn looked uncomfortable for a moment, then said, "Alicia, I hope you'll let me spend time with Emily while you're here. I've wanted a grandchild for so long."

Alicia smiled at the older woman and said sincerely, "Of course you can spend time with her. I'm not sure exactly what Jon has planned, but we can't be on the go the whole time."

Marilyn beamed. "He said you're staying two weeks."

"That's all I can be away right now." Alicia took two glasses from the cupboard. "Would you like a glass of soda or juice, Mrs. Wescott?"

"Please call me Marilyn. And, no, I don't need anything right now. Why don't we go sit down. In Jon's not-too-subtle way he's trying to let us get acquainted."

They went into the living room and settled on the sofa. Alicia glanced around the room again, trying to get used to her surroundings.

"Not the furnishings I'd choose for a house with children," Marilyn commented. "Maybe Jon will make some changes."

If she didn't move to California, Jon would probably want Emily in the summers. How could Alicia stand being away from her daughter that long? How could she stand being that far from Jon?

Marilyn tilted her head and studied Alicia with the same intensity Jon sometimes used. "Jon called me with the results of the paternity test."

"He was sure he was Emily's father before the results came through. And when I stopped fighting the idea, so was I. She has his eyes, his cheekbones."

Marilyn added, "His smile."

Alicia nodded. "I'm still not sure what's going to happen. In a sense, Jon's holding all the cards. If I don't move out here, I'd have to be separated from Emily. And if we do move out here..."

"Everything you know and love is in Pennsylvania."

"You understand?"

"Certainly. Jon tells me you have a twin sister you're close to."

Alicia curled one leg under her, appreciating the smooth buttery leather against her calf. "I'm not sure close is the right word. We almost know what the other is thinking."

"I don't envy you your decision. But I do want to tell you that if you move here, I'll do everything I can to make the transition easier for you. I'm sure Jon will, too."

Jon. How could she go back to Pennsylvania and only see him intermittently?

Marilyn continued, "I've never heard Jon as happy as in these past weeks he's been in Pennsylvania. I was worried about him. I think Emily has given him new purpose in his life. I hope now that he's back he doesn't start working twenty hours a day again."

"He's a good father. And he spends as much time as he can with her. When she's here, I think she'll be the priority."

"And when she's here, will you be here? I mean if you don't move?"

"We haven't discussed that yet. I trust him with Emily, but I don't know how much time I'm willing to spend away from her. Yet I have a business to run. It's a complicated situation."

Marilyn canvassed Alicia's face. "I can see that."

Alicia guessed Marilyn could see more than the situation, that she might suspect Alicia had feelings for her son.

Adam Hobbs's house was twice as big as Jon's. Jon had told Alicia that not only did Adam and his wife, Jana, have a year-old baby, but that his two daughters from a previous marriage also stayed with them on and off. When Jon had asked her if she'd like to go to a pool party at Adam's, she figured she might as well jump in with both feet and get to know Jon's friends. Now, on Adam's patio, her white terry wrap firmly knotted at the waist, she wondered what she'd been thinking.

Adam and Jana had greeted them at the door. The couple had been friendly and welcoming. Alicia and Jon had mingled for a while and then changed into their swimsuits in separate bedrooms. Jon must have gotten waylaid somewhere because he wasn't in the room where he'd changed or on the patio. Looking around, Alicia went to the bar for a glass of white wine and studied her surroundings. Many of the women on the patio wore bikinis, all wore suits that probably cost more than her profits for a week. Her own suit, a black satiny maillot, could be found on more than one rack at any department store. She'd purchased it on sale at the end of a season.

Not feeling as if she could just go up to strangers and start a conversation, she sat at one of the tables. Adam saw her, crossed to her and sat down. "Well, what do you think?"

She wasn't sure what to think about Adam. Jon said he was treacherous in corporate negotiations. His blue eyes twinkled with friendliness, but his squared jaw hinted at an aggressive attitude she supposed could surface in a second.

"About?" she asked in answer to his question.

"California, of course."

She took a sip of wine and set down her glass. "I've only seen a small bit of it. Jon's house, the beach, the observatory, Disneyland. He did say he's taking me to Rodeo Drive tomorrow."

Adam's gaze seemed to take in everything about her, from the flutter of her finger against her glass to the tilt of her head. It wasn't male interest; it was lawyer interest. She had the distinct feeling he was sizing her up. "To buy something for the charity gala?" he guessed.

"You and Jon must think alike. Unless you're a mind reader."

"Or else Jon told me yesterday when I asked him to the party."

To divert Adam's attention from her, she commented, "You have a lovely house."

"It's nice, and big, and since I married Jana, it's become a real home."

Alicia relaxed a bit. "Jon said your little boy was a year old last week."

"He took his first steps yesterday." Adam's voice held the awe of a proud father. "I wanted to keep Matthew up to show him off, but Jana insisted he'd enjoy our parties more when he gets older."

Alicia smiled. "I remember Emily's first steps."

"How does Emily like it out here?" Adam asked casually.

Alicia would bet that swimming pool he'd already asked Jon the same question. "She seems to have adapted easily. She loves the beach. It's one big sandbox. She's afraid of the ocean, but Jon helped her get a few toes wet this afternoon."

Adam leaned back in his chair, resting his hands on the arms. "I suppose Marilyn is baby-sitting tonight?"

"Yes. Do you know her well?"

He chuckled. "For years. She's given me guiding lectures now and then."

"Did you need them?"

His blue eyes flickered with amusement. "Probably."

Jon pushed open the sliding glass door and stepped outside. Alicia stared and stared some more. She'd seen his bare chest before. But add bare hairy legs, muscled thighs and a pair of navy trunks that hugged him too well, and she couldn't swallow let alone breathe.

He opened the gate leading to the pool. "Are you bothering the lady, Hobbs?"

"Am I bothering you, Alicia?"

Somehow she found her voice. "No, you're protecting Jon's interests."

The two men looked at each other. Adam shook his head. "She's sharp. Here I thought I was being subtle." Pushing his chair in, he faced Alicia. "Don't blame Jon. We've known each other a long time and I'm more than his lawyer, I'm his friend."

As Adam moved away to talk to other guests, Jon sat beside her. "Did he give you the third degree?" His question was edged with annoyance at his friend.

"No. Like he said, he was subtle."

"I'll talk to him."

"That's not necessary. You don't have to protect me, Jon."

He smiled and fingered a strand of her hair curling on the lapel of her robe. "Are you sure?"

She smiled back. "I'm sure."

"Are you going to swim with me?"

The women standing around the pool looked as if the last thing they wanted to do was get their suits or hair wet. But the balmy night, the unearthly blue lights under the water, Jon beside her, beckoned. She took a deep breath. "Sure."

Jon watched as her hands went to the belt of her wraparound. Loosening the knot, she unbelted it and the lapels fell open. Jon's green eyes heated with the sensual awareness that always hummed between them. Chills broke out on her arms, but she shrugged out of the robe anyway.

His slow, sexy smile chased the chills away. His gaze flicked from her halter top, to her slim waist, to her long legs. He held out his hand and she took it.

Jon swam laps while Alicia floated on her back. No one else was in the pool. She let bits of stray conversation and laughter float around her until a hand grabbed her ankle and she yelped. Before she knew it, Jon's hands were around her waist and he was holding her in front of him.

She gripped his shoulders—strong, hard, wet shoulders—and tried to tear her gaze from the droplets of water collected in his chest hair. "I thought you were going to swim for a while."

He grimaced, his frustration laced with the tight edge of desire. "How in blazes am I supposed to swim when all I can see in front of my eyes is the way you look in this suit?"

"But it's sedate."

"It's sexy as sin."

"I'm covered," she blurted out.

Sliding his hands up from her waist to under her arms, from there down to the tops of her thighs, he murmured, "You sure are. And I'm imagining exactly how you look underneath."

She felt the heat flow to her face and couldn't do anything about it. "Jon."

He tipped her chin up and stroked her cheek. "Right now, I want to strip that suit off you and look at every lovely inch. And then I want to touch every lovely inch. If that embarrasses you, I'm sorry, but that's all I can think about lately." He pulled her even closer until she fit against him. Her softness molded to his hardness, and the titillating temptation even with their clothes on shortened her breath.

Jon's eyes seemed to pierce her with a knowing intensity that aroused everything womanly within her. The trembling around her heart swept lower and wider. She felt three beats of his heart before he lowered his head and took her lips in a devouring kiss that sent a string of tremors through her. With masculine demand, he parted her lips with his tongue. As darkness surrounded them except for the blue underwater lights, with all the guests sitting on the patio talking and drinking, they seemed to be alone in a sensual world of water and touch, heat and a slight breeze. There was Jon and need and love.

Jon's hand slipped between them. She felt his palm on her breast as he deepened the kiss. Arching into him, she forgot they were at Adam's house, she forgot she should be cautious, she forgot that she didn't know if he loved her. When his thumb stroked across her nipple, she pushed her thighs against his, felt his hardness, and accepted it, reveled in it, rocked against him until he tore his mouth from hers and groaned her name.

Moving his hands again to her waist, he bowed his forehead against hers. "My God, Alicia, I could take you right here."

Her racing heart tightened her throat. Sucking in a puff of air, she could still taste Jon, could still smell Jon, could still feel every tingle from his body molded to hers. "I don't think Adam would appreciate it."

"The hell with Adam," he growled.

She smiled and kissed him lightly on the lips. "He's your friend."

Jon sighed and raised his head. No one seemed to notice them standing near the deep end at the side of the pool. To anyone on the patio, it looked as if they were having an intense conversation. He'd never do anything to compromise Alicia's reputation, but he wanted her more than he'd ever wanted anything in his life.

When they left the party, they were both silent as he drove home. He pulled the car into the garage, then said, "Let's take a walk on the beach."

"Don't you think we should tell your mom we're back?"

"I think she'll guess. She heard the garage door go up."

Jon took Alicia's hand as they walked down the stone steps to the beach area. Her sandals clicked against the stone, but Jon's sneakers were silent. The roar of the ocean in the distance echoed like a benevolent rumble of thunder. The *swish* and *swoosh* of the surf soothed the line between sand and horizon.

They'd walked for a while when he said, "You and Mom seem to get along well."

"I like her. Very much. So does Emily."

He stopped and tried to see Alicia in the glow of the moon. "You're not just saying that."

"Have I ever lied to you?"

A ghost of a smile slipped across his lips. "No. Come to think of it, you don't even gloss the truth." His heart felt lighter and he wasn't sure why he felt so relieved. He lightly swung her hand as the sand slid around his sneakers. "Emily makes her smile and laugh. She hasn't done enough of that since Dad died."

"Do you think she'll ever remarry?"

He was shocked for a moment. "I honestly never thought about it."

"She's an attractive lady. With all the charity work she does, she could easily meet someone."

"I hope she docs. She's always wanted to travel. Dad would never take the time away from work." He'd been thinking about his parents a lot lately. But he'd been thinking about something else more. "How do you like the ocean?"

"It's wonderful. It's amazing that you have it in your front yard. You're very lucky."

He stopped again and took hold of her shoulders. "I'd like to be even luckier. You've been here a week. What do you think? Could you be happy living in Los Angeles?"

She hesitated, then answered, "Truthfully, I've postponed thinking about it. I do know one thing for sure. I don't want to give up my business."

Some part of him had been holding its breath, had been worrying about Alicia's reaction to his house, the city where he lived. He didn't want Emily with him on a sometimes basis, he wanted her here all the time. And the picture wasn't complete without Alicia. He stroked her hair away from her cheek. "I can understand that. Why don't we look at a few office spaces tomorrow?" He'd do everything in his power to lure her to the West Coast.

"All right."

Seeing the doubt and confusion in her eyes, he thought he knew what they came from. Ria would still be in Camp Hill. So would her friends and everything she'd known all her life. He couldn't push this decision, but he could make her want it as much as he did.

Taking her in his arms, he kissed her. The breeze blew, the surf rolled, the sand shifted and Jon knew he couldn't let Alicia and Emily fly out of his life.

The next afternoon, Adam's message didn't alarm Jon, but it did make him wonder what was so urgent. "Come to my office as soon as you get in. It's important."

Jon had taken Alicia through a few office spaces before they went shopping. She hadn't seemed impressed. Something was troubling her. Maybe it was more than leaving Ria in Camp Hill. Maybe she simply didn't like the idea of surf and sand twelve months of the year.

She'd seemed excited when they'd picked up his mother and gone shopping. He'd taken Emily to a nearby park while the women explored the dress shops. Now Emily was taking a nap, and her mother and grandmother were *oohing* and *aahing* over their purchases.

Peeking into the guest bedroom, barely noticing a froth of pink on the bed, he said, "I'm stopping at Adam's then going into the office for a few hours. If you need me, that's where I'll be."

His mother waved him away. "We're fine. Alicia and I will see what we can concoct for supper. Unless . . . I'm sorry I'm pushing in. If you want to be alone, I'll understand."

Yes, he wanted to be alone with Alicia, but he understood his mother's need to be around them. Glancing at Alicia, he saw her small smile of understanding. "You're more than welcome to stay for supper. I'll take you home afterward."

He couldn't forget his mother's pleased and happy expression as he drove to Adam's office. The secretary buzzed Adam when Jon arrived and the lawyer told her to send him in.

Adam took off his wire-rimmed glasses as Jon approached his desk. "We've got trouble with a capital *T*."

"What kind of trouble?"

"Valerie Sentara."

"She's just a nuisance."

"She managed to get my most recent paralegal to divulge some information."

"About?"

"You and Alicia. This is the same paralegal who typed up your letter of intent to file for visitation rights."

Jon's epithet was loud and harsh enough to carry through the closed door.

"I'm sorry. Valerie called me this morning to give me the chance to verify. Can you imagine the gall of that woman? I told her to take a hike, and she said the article comes out Monday on the Style page. She even gave me the headline. Newspaper Tycoon Claims Illegitimate Daughter."

Rage percolated through Jon until slamming his hand through the wall seemed to be the only option.

Adam looked at him with concern. "Want a drink? I have some scotch."

Jon ignored his friend's offer. "I will not have Emily and Alicia put smack dab in the middle of a scandal. If I could get my hands around that woman's neck—"

"You'd go to prison for murder one. Try to calm down, Jon. We can think our way out of this. You know we can."

"For God's sake, Adam, this isn't some math problem we can solve. That woman's a walking time bomb!"

"Yes, she is. But there has got to be some way we can defuse her."

Jon went to Adam's window, the same window he remembered staring out of after he'd learned he had a daughter. His mind started clicking and the solution suddenly became obvious. "I'll ask Alicia to marry me. Tonight. We'll get it out to the other newspapers, then call Ms. Sentara. If everybody else is writing about the wedding of a newspaper tycoon, the emphasis will be on that, not Emily. It will take the wind out of Sentara's sails. She doesn't like happy endings, she likes scandals."

Adam's brows arched. "Are you sure this is what you want to do? Marriage is a big step."

It didn't seem like such a big step. Subconsciously he must have been considering it for some time or it wouldn't seem like the natural solution it was now. "This is what I want to do. Alicia and I are good together."

"Are you doing this because you want a life with Alicia or because you don't want to be separated from Emily?"

"Both. Now all I have to do is to convince Alicia."

After Alicia put Emily to bed, she waited for Jon to come back from taking his mother home. Tomorrow night was the charity gala. She couldn't wait for Jon to see her in the dress she'd purchased. She'd paid much too much. But she wanted Jon to be proud of her. More than that, she wanted to see the desire leap into his eyes when he looked at her. Maybe she'd even see love.

She heard the garage door. When Jon came in, he sat down on the sofa next to her. "Is Emily all tucked in?"

"When we get back, she's going to sleep for a week. There's so much to see and do while she's here, she's afraid to close her eyes. She might miss something."

"Maybe she won't have to miss anything."

Jon was talking about more than sightseeing. Alicia's pulse raced.

He took something out of his pocket. It was a small velvet box. Opening it, he asked, "Will you marry me?"

The marquise diamond was recessed in a wide band of gold. She'd never seen a diamond that large it had to be at least two karats. Meeting his gaze, her mouth went dry. She wanted more than anything in the world to say yes, to be his wife, to stand beside him, to be joined to him forever. But why did he want to marry her? Because he desired her? Or because he loved her? Or because of Emily?

Only one of those was the basis Alicia wanted for a marriage.

"If you don't like it, we can pick out another one."

The ring was the last thing on her mind. "Oh, no. It's beautiful. It's just . . ."

"You're not sure. Alicia, we'd have a good life. Emily would have the best of everything. You would, too. And I know how much you'd miss Ria, but you can fly back anytime you want. And we can fly her out."

Not a word about love. Pride made her unable to ask. Pride made her say, "Give me some time to think about it."

His gaze became shuttered, the nerve in his jaw worked. "We need to settle this, Alicia. For all our sakes. You know I'll be good to you and Emily."

She needed time to think. She needed time to decide whether her love for Jon was enough or if she needed to hear him say the words and mean them. "I'll give you my answer tomorrow night. After the gala."

He looked almost relieved. "The ring is yours whether you say yes or no." He tipped her face toward him and smoothed his thumb along her cheek. "But I want you to say yes, more than I've ever wanted anything in my life."

Was that love she heard? Or was it the hope in her heart thinking she heard it?

Chapter Ten

Saturday night, Alicia touched the pink chiffon swirling elegantly over her hips. Feeling a little like Cinderella at the ball, she smiled at a comment someone made to the group of women standing with her in the immense foyer of the Wescott Industries office complex. Marilyn had insisted she'd baby-sit Emily tonight. She'd assured Alicia that spending time with her granddaughter was much more important than catching up on the latest gossip.

Soon after they'd arrived at the charity gala, Jon had been monopolized by colleagues, guests and advertisers. Alicia understood this was a business function for him, and in a way, she was grateful she didn't have to deal with his intense regard, his questioning looks. Because she still didn't have an answer for him. She didn't know if she was ready to settle for a marriage with passion but without Jon's love.

Someone tapped her on the shoulder. Alicia turned to face a woman dressed in black. Her four-inch spike heels brought the top of her head to Alicia's nose. Her long straight hair swept over one bare shoulder. Extending her hand, the woman said, "Hello, Mrs. Fallon. I'm Valerie Sentara. Could I talk to you for a few minutes?"

Alicia recognized the smoky voice as well as the name. "I don't think that would be a good idea."

"I know about your adopted daughter, Jonathan Wescott's daughter. My article comes out Monday with or without your verification."

The horrified fear in Alicia's heart must have shown on her face.

"You didn't know about the article? I'm sure Adam Hobbs told Jon after I called him."

Alicia tried to absorb the information that was coming so quickly.

Valerie pressed on. "Cecile Braddock was the mother's name, correct?"

Alicia calmed herself so she could think. "Where did you get your information?"

"One source leads to another. It's not as difficult as you might think. Reporters have the same skills as PI's. There's a lounge off the foyer. Why don't we go there and talk." She took Alicia's arm to lead her off.

Alicia pulled back and didn't move a step. "We don't have anything to talk about. Just make sure you print the truth or we'll sue."

The reporter ran her eyes over Alicia, trying to measure her clout. "Let me run the truth by you. Jonathan Wescott has an illegitimate child he has not supported since her birth. He ran her mother out of town—"

"Wrong facts, Ms. Sentara," Jon interrupted in a sharp voice. "Print that and we will sue. You don't care about truth, you care about spreading rumors. Well, you've gotten hold of the wrong one this time. Every other newspaper in the area will be running the announcement of my engagement to Mrs. Fallon tomorrow. Emily will be a side issue. But you don't care about stories that turn out well, do you?"

He took the program from the inside pocket of his tuxedo jacket and tapped it on his palm. "This is a private function, Ms. Sentara. I advise you to find your way out before I do it for you."

The reporter's face was a mask, but she knew Jon's threat was a serious one. "An engagement, huh? What do you know?" She gave Jon and Alicia a curt nod and said, "You can't say I don't try," and walked toward the exit with her back straight.

Alicia couldn't decide if she was more hurt or angry. She did know she was devastated, as if all hope was gone. Jon had asked her to marry him for one reason. And it wasn't love. Keeping her voice even and controlled, she said, "I have to talk to you."

He took one look at her expression and agreed. "There's a room upstairs we can use."

Alicia had difficulty putting one foot in front of the other. Because she knew what she had to do. The flight of steps seemed like Mount Everest. In silence, Jon ushered her to an elegantly appointed office. Before he closed the door behind them, she reached into her purse and took out the small velvet box.

She held it out to him. "I can't accept this."

He was immobile, except for the nerve on his jaw that spoke of his controlled emotion. "I told you it was yours whether you said yes or no."

Reaching for his hand, the touch of him almost making her cry, she set the box in his palm. "I can't accept this because it was a bribe, your offer of a handy solution. Why didn't you tell me about the article?''

He closed his hand around the box slowly. "I didn't want to upset you. I was heading her off—"

"By asking me to marry you," she said flatly, wishing it wasn't true.

"Yes, but—"

Her voice rose as her hurt got the best of her. "There are no buts. I love you, Jon. I love you more than I thought I could ever love any man. But you want to get married for all the wrong reasons. Because of the article, because of Emily. We can't build a future on that."

"Of course, we can," he said angrily. "If you don't accept, she'll print that damn garbage."

"I don't care about the article. No, I don't want Emily in the middle of a scandal any more than you do. But I'm not going to marry you to prevent it. If the article goes to press, I'll deal with it."

"You have no idea of the reporters who will be on your doorstep."

She waved the idea away. "I'll handle them. It'll blow over in a day or two. A week or two. Or are you more important than that?"

He swore and clenched his fists at his sides. "No, I'm not more important than that. I didn't want you subjected to the fishbowl. Especially with what she wanted to print. Alicia, you have to understand I would have proposed anyway, eventually. Valerie just gave me a reason to do it sooner."

"You would have proposed because you want the right kind of family for Emily. Because you want to protect her and take care of her. Well, so do I. But not like this."

"Alicia . . ."

"Don't you understand I feel betrayed? Belittled? You should have told me what was happening. We should have decided *together* what to do. My marriage to Patrick might not have been passionate, but we had honesty between us. I don't want a marriage of convenience. I want a true, loving partnership."

A haunting sadness filled Jon's eyes. "I thought I was doing what was best for everyone."

She tried to soothe her aching heart with logic as she fought her tears. "What's best is for me to take Emily back to Pennsylvania. As soon as I can. I'll take a taxi back to the house."

"You will not. I'll take you back. But you're not leaving until we talk about this, until you realize you can trust me."

"Trust you? To what? Keep things from me? That's not my idea of trust. We don't have anything else to talk about, Jon. You stay and take care of business. It'll be easier for both of us." She hurried out the door before her tears fell.

When Jon returned home, he found the note from his mother on the refrigerator next to a drawing Emily had colored of the ocean. It said simply that she'd taken Alicia to the airport. His stomach churned, his chest hurt and the pounding in his ears was as loud as the ocean at high tide. As loud as Alicia's voice as she'd said she loved him. His heart clenched on the thought.

He wanted to lash out, hit, swear, but he knew he had no one to blame for this debacle but himself. He'd told Alicia he liked to take charge. Well, he'd taken charge right out of her life.

Going to the cabinet under the stereo in the living room, he took out a bottle of whiskey that had been there since he moved in. The small shot glass glimmered in the lamplight as he sat on the sofa and filled it to the brim. The liquor's searing heat burned his throat. As soon as Alicia had walked away from him, he'd known he had to let her go. He had to give her the freedom to choose to stay or go. And she'd gone. The pain was almost unbearable. The loss ate at him until he rested his head against the sofa and closed his eyes.

He didn't know how long he'd been sitting there, gazing out the picture window into the moonless night, when his mother opened the door. He should have expected she'd come back here rather than going home. He should have expected she'd want an explanation.

Without speaking, she came in, dropped her purse on the coffee table and sat in the chair across from him. Seeing the bottle of whiskey, she asked, "How many did you have?"

"One. God knows I'd like to down the bottle. But you and I both know that won't solve any problems."

Her tone was sympathetic. "No, it won't."

"What did Alicia tell you?" he asked gruffly, not blaming her if she'd raked him over the coals.

"Nothing. Just that she had to go home right away. When she found out there was a flight tonight, I couldn't have kept her here if I'd chained her."

No recriminations. No demanding an explanation. His mother waited as she had when he was a teenager and had gotten himself into trouble. Raking his hand through his hair, he said, "I blew it."

"Meaning?"

"My chances with Alicia. I've been so careful with her, so damn patient."

"Why?"

He was quiet for a moment. "Because I wanted to get closer to her."

"You mean you wanted to get close to Emily."

"No, that's not what I mean. From the first moment I saw Alicia, there was this freshness about her. A vulnerability wrapped in strength that intrigued me."

"I see."

He went on as if explaining it to himself. "She's got this smile I can see when I close my eyes, and she challenges me. She doesn't accept everything I say without question. I can see spending the rest of my life with her so clearly..."

"In other words, you love her," Marilyn said quietly.

He thought about the words. He thought about the myriad feelings he had every time he was with Alicia—the warmth, the desire, the respect, the need. And he'd been afraid to call it love. Because of Cecile?

That didn't matter now. Only Alicia mattered and the life they could have together. "She won't believe me if I say it. Not now. She thinks I want to marry her because of Emily. And Emily's certainly part of it. But only because Alicia's such a wonderful mother. I love her for herself, not because she's Emily's mother. How can I get her to believe that?"

"You asked Alicia to marry you without telling her you loved her?" Marilyn asked, aghast.

He pushed himself off the sofa and paced to the window. "All right. So I'm an idiot. I knew I wanted to marry her, I just didn't realize..."

"That you loved her. Just like your father."

Jon turned at that.

"He couldn't say the words. They were so hard for him. And I guess you never heard them spoken between us, though I said them in private to him. But I knew he loved me."

"How did you know?"

"By what he did. How he cared for me. And if you give Alicia some time, maybe she'll realize it, too. Your dreams aren't gone, Jon. They might just be postponed for a while."

Patience was not his strong suit. But this time he couldn't take charge. He had to wait for some sign from Alicia that she was ready to listen. Because when she was, he was going to give her an earful, every whisper an "I love you." He might even be willing to shout it if he had to. Whatever was necessary to make her believe he loved her for herself.

Alicia was making a list of all the supplies she'd need for Emily's birthday party when her daughter came running to the kitchen table with a picture in her hands. "See what I drew?"

Alicia took her daughter onto her lap. "Tell me all about it."

"It's you and me and Daddy."

Alicia's eyes misted over as they always did when she thought about Jon. It had been four days since she'd flown home. A miserable four days. There'd been no word from Jon. In fact, no word from anybody on the West Coast. Valerie Sentara hadn't tried to reach her, nor had any other reporter. That puzzled Alicia, but she was relieved she didn't have to deal with the press, too. Emily had asked enough questions for all of them. Why had they left? When were they going back? Was her Daddy coming to see her soon?

Alicia answered truthfully that she didn't know any of the answers and tried to distract Emily from missing Jon.

She hoped she was more successful with her daughter than she had been with herself. Nothing could distract her from thinking about Jon.

Tears welled in her eyes. Blinking the moisture away so she could examine Emily's picture, she pointed to each figure's shoulders. "What are these?"

"Can't you tell? They're wings! So all of us can fly from here to *Cal-i-for-nya* and from *Cal-i-for-nya* here whenever we want. Then I won't miss Daddy and he won't miss you and me."

The wings of fate had brought Jon to them. Emily missed him as much as Alicia did. She wondered what he was thinking. Did he fear she'd keep Emily from him now? She could never do that; she knew it would hurt him. No matter how it would hurt her, she knew, he deserved joint custody. With things the way they were between them, maybe he'd sue for sole custody!

The thought scared her enough to make her say, "I have to make a phone call, honey. Why don't you draw another picture you can send to Daddy."

Emily ran to the living room, and Alicia went to the phone. She'd called Adam's number once before. Flicking it out of her wallet, she dialed. Adam's secretary put her through. His hello was businesslike.

"This is Alicia Fallon."

"Yes, my secretary told me. What can I do for you?" he asked politely.

"I'd like you to give a message to Jon. Tell him I won't fight joint custody. I hate the idea of being away from Emily, but maybe Jon will agree to having her in Los Angeles during summers with visits in between."

She could hear Adam's sigh through the line. "Jon's not suing for any custody, Alicia. He believes Emily belongs with you. But he does want to visit under whatever conditions you set up.''

Relief poured over her like a soothing balm. ''I'm grateful Jon loves Emily enough to put her first.''

Adam hesitated then added, ''He's thinking of you, too, Alicia. He cares for you as much as he cares for Emily. It's a shame you can't see that.''

Adam's statement left her speechless. After a mumbled thank you and goodbye, she hung up. Could it be true? Could Jon care about her as much as he cared about his daughter even though he hadn't said it? How did Adam know? Had Jon told him?

Alicia thought about the time she'd spent with Jon from the first moment he'd appeared on her doorstep. The picnic supper. The vase. Helping her when she was swamped. His kisses. His hugs. His desire. Opening his home to her. Were her own insecurities keeping her from seeing the truth?

There was only one way to find out. She had to risk asking him. Face-to-face. So she could see his expression, and gaze into his eyes. She had the perfect opportunity—Emily's birthday party. With her heart pounding, she picked up the phone again. Checking her watch, she realized it was late morning in California. Hopefully he'd be in his office.

Again she had to go through a receptionist. She could hardly swallow as she waited. Finally he answered. ''Alicia?''

Keeping her voice steady, she said, ''I'm having a birthday party for Emily on Saturday evening. Would you like to fly in for it?''

His silence scared her.

''I'll understand if you're busy—''

''I'm not busy. What time?''

"Oh, around seven, but you're welcome to come earlier."

"I'll check the flights and let you know."

She didn't know what else to say. "That's fine."

"Alicia?"

"Mmm-hmm."

"Thanks for inviting me."

After he said goodbye and hung up, she smiled. Maybe risks weren't so bad. Maybe she could thank fate and believe in dreams.

Saturday evening, Alicia checked her appearance in a violet-colored romper as well as her watch every five minutes as five six-year-olds besides Emily played Simon Says in her living room. Just as one little girl raised her hand above her head when Simon in the form of Ria didn't say to do it, and all the girls pointed and squealed, the doorbell rang. Alicia hurried to the door and opened it.

Jon, dressed in yellow slacks and a white polo shirt, looking more handsome than she'd ever seen him, stepped inside with three presents tied with pink and white bows stacked up in front of him. "Sorry, I'm late. Flight was delayed." His green gaze seemed to swallow her as she absorbed his presence again in her home.

"We waited for you to have the birthday cake. But I'm sure Emily will want to open her presents first."

"Daddy! Daddy! Mommy told me you were coming."

He dumped the presents on a chair and lifted his daughter into his arms. "Hi, kiddo. How about a great big hug?"

Her daughter squeezed Jon, and Alicia wished she could do the same. Her nerves were rioting, but she knew she probably wouldn't have a chance to talk to Jon until the party was over.

As Emily opened the doll and radio-controlled car from Jon and the horse with a long mane and tail that she could comb from Marilyn, Jon's gaze caught Alicia's. She thought she saw longing in his eyes, but she couldn't be sure. She wasn't sure of anything tonight. Except that she loved him and she was going to find out if he loved her.

Emily blew out her candles and Alicia cut the cake. Everything seemed to take forever. Finally when each child sat at the kitchen table with a piece of cake, assorted snacks and juice, Ria came up beside Alicia and said, "Go down to your office. I'll take care of these imps."

Glancing around, Alicia didn't see Jon and suspected he was waiting downstairs. Her hands grew clammy as she descended the steps.

Jon was standing by her desk, waiting. She stopped in front of him, close enough to smell his cologne, close enough to touch him.

"I was surprised when you called," he said, studying her expression, maybe trying to gauge her mood.

"I made a mistake leaving the way I did." She'd come to that conclusion after her phone call to him.

"Maybe not."

Her hope withered. If Jon was glad she'd left . . .

"It made me look at some things more carefully."

"What things?" she asked, sounding breathless.

"First of all, you were right to be angry about the article. I should have told you. My only excuse is that I did want to protect you, and I grabbed onto the situation as the reason to ask you to marry me. I couldn't recognize love even though it was filling me up until I thought I'd overflow. I called it everything but. By the time I'd realized just how much I love you, you'd left, and I knew you weren't ready to listen, you'd think I was manipulating you to get what I want.''

Her heart almost stopped. ''I'm ready to listen.''

He grasped her shoulders. ''I love our daughter, Alicia. But I love you, too. I never heard my parents say they loved each other, and they weren't demonstrative. It was just understood. They had this bond, and I could feel the same bond forming with us. But I didn't associate it with love. After Cecile, I decided I'd never feel deeply about anyone again. But I knew something was happening with you. And I knew we could have a future. I was just afraid to call it love, I guess. Can you believe me now when I say I love you?''

The raw need on Jon's face was as convincing as his words. Alicia couldn't stop the tears from falling down her cheeks. ''Yes, I can believe you. I love you, Jon. And after I talked to Adam, I realized you'd shown me love over and over again. Maybe I was afraid to see it, too. My own insecurities blinded me. But I can see it now, and if your proposal still stands—''

He closed her in his arms and sought her lips with all the hunger of the past week evident in his kiss. He was tender and demanding, gentle and passionate, devouring and teasing. She pressed against him, wanting all of him and everything he could give her. She had no more doubts, no more fears. His love had wiped them away.

Breaking the kiss, he rested his cheek against hers for a moment, then raised his head. ''I want to get married as soon as we can arrange it.''

She lifted her head. ''But, Jon, we live three thousand miles apart. . . .''

He smiled. "Not for long. How would you feel about living here during the school year, maybe flying out to L.A. for Thanksgiving and Christmas with Mom, and then living at the beach house in the summers? With fax machines, there's no reason why you can't run your business from L.A. for the summer, though you might want to cut down then." He straightened a little. "This doesn't sound as if I'm running your life, does it? I mean, it's open for discussion."

Taking his face between her palms, she placed an ineffably tender kiss on his lips and felt the shudder that forked through him. "It's a wonderful idea. But what about you?"

He stroked her back and brought his hands up to play in her hair. "Wescott Industries has been considering acquiring a few East Coast papers. I can open a corporate office here. I might have to fly out to L.A. now and then, but I think it'll work well."

"You've thought of everything."

"Except how to put a gag on Valerie Sentara. After the confrontation at the gala, she didn't know what to print. When no engagement announcement appeared in the other papers, she called me. I told her if she gave me two weeks, I'd give her an exclusive interview and she could print the complete version of the story."

"Two weeks?"

"That's all the time I was going to give you before I took some action. You don't think I'd let you shut me out of your life, do you?"

The love in Jon's eyes was so overwhelming, her throat tightened. She stroked his jaw because she couldn't find any words.

He gave her an understanding smile. "So are you going to do the interview with me?"

The idea wasn't totally pleasant. "What if she's combative?"

"I'll handle her." He amended, "*We'll* handle her." As he gently let Alicia's hair flow through his fingers, he said, "As I see it, we only have one problem now to contend with."

"And what's that?"

"We have to convince Ria to let us fly her out to L.A. for holidays. Think she'll come?"

"If the rest of our problems are that easy to solve, we'll have a wonderful life."

"We will have a wonderful life. And every day for the rest of it, I'm going to bless the fates who put Emily in your care. I love you, Alicia."

She raised her lips to his for another kiss, a kiss that showed him she believed him, she loved him, and she'd be his for always.

*   *   *   *   *

*The DARLING DADDIES series continues
with SHANE'S BRIDE, coming soon from
Silhouette Romance.*

COMING NEXT MONTH

#1108 THE DAD NEXT DOOR—Kasey Michaels
Fabulous Fathers
Quinn Patrick moved in only to find trouble next door—in the form of lovely neighbor Maddie Pemberton and her son, Dillon. Was this confirmed bachelor about to end up with a ready-made family?

#1109 TEMPORARILY HERS—Susan Meier
Bundles of Joy
Katherine Whitman was determined to win custody of her nephew Jason—even if it meant a temporary marriage to playboy Alex Cane. Then Katherine found herself falling for her new "husband" and facing permanent heartache.

#1110 STAND-IN HUSBAND—Anne Peters
Pavel Mallik remembered nothing. All he knew was that the lovely Marie Cooper had saved his life. Now he had the chance to rescue her reputation by making her his wife!

#1111 STORYBOOK COWBOY—Pat Montana
Jo McPherson didn't trust Trey Covington. The handsome cowboy brought back too many memories. Jo tried to resist his charm, but Trey had his ways of making her forget the past...and dream about the future.

#1112 FAMILY TIES—Dani Criss
Single mother Laine Sullivan knew Drew Casteel was commitment shy. It would be smarter to steer clear of the handsome bachelor. But Drew was hard to resist. Soon Laine had to decide whether or not to risk her heart....

#1113 HONEYMOON SUITE—Linda Lewis
Premiere
Miranda St. James had always been pursued for her celebrity connections. So when Stuart Winslow began to woo her, Miranda kept her identity a secret. But Stuart had secrets of his own!

Take 4 bestselling love stories FREE

Plus get a FREE surprise gift!

Special Limited-time Offer

Mail to Silhouette Reader Service™

3010 Walden Avenue
P.O. Box 1867
Buffalo, N.Y. 14269-1867

YES! Please send me 4 free Silhouette Romance™ novels and my free surprise gift. Then send me 6 brand-new novels every month, which I will receive months before they appear in bookstores. Bill me at the low price of $2.19 each plus 25¢ delivery and applicable sales tax, if any.* That's the complete price and a savings of over 10% off the cover prices—quite a bargain! I understand that accepting the books and gift places me under no obligation ever to buy any books. I can always return a shipment and cancel at any time. Even if I never buy another book from Silhouette, the 4 free books and the surprise gift are mine to keep forever.

215 BPA ANRP

Name	(PLEASE PRINT)	
Address	Apt. No.	
City	State	Zip

This offer is limited to one order per household and not valid to present Silhouette Romance™ subscribers. *Terms and prices are subject to change without notice. Sales tax applicable in N.Y.

Become a *Privileged Woman*, *You'll* be entitled to all these *Free Benefits.* And *Free Gifts*, too.

To thank you for buying our books, we've designed an exclusive FREE program called *PAGES & PRIVILEGES™*. You can enroll with just one Proof of Purchase, and get the kind of luxuries that, until now, you could only read about.

Big HOTEL DISCOUNTS

A privileged woman stays in the finest hotels. And so can you—at up to 60% off! Imagine standing in a hotel check-in line and watching as the guest in front of you pays $150 for the same room that's only costing you $60. Your *Pages & Privileges* discounts are good at Sheraton, Marriott, Best Western, Hyatt and thousands of other fine hotels all over the U.S., Canada and Europe.

Free DISCOUNT TRAVEL SERVICE

A privileged woman is always jetting to romantic places.

When <u>you</u> fly, just make one phone call for the lowest published airfare at time of booking— <u>or double the difference back!</u>

PLUS—you'll get a $25 voucher to use the first time you book a flight AND <u>5% cash back on every ticket you buy thereafter through the travel service!</u>